The beach disgorged them onto the sea

Nate Beck revved up the engines, and they began to ease away. He turned the boat toward the open sea and away from the plumes of smoke drifting from the black volcanic peaks behind them.

Claude Hayes twisted around for a squinty-eyed look and suddenly shouted, "God almighty!"

Barrabas and the others craned their necks to gaze at the man standing at the top of the island's plateau. It had to be Billy Two—no one else had a build that looked like his.

Billy Two spread out his arms and began to bend his knees, preparing to jump from that impossible height into the blue Pacific.

"Does he think he can fly?" Claude screamed, then they watched in silent awe as Billy Two leaped into the air, his legs straight, arms outstretched, his head in perfect alignment with his body. For a heartbeat the Indian seemed perfectly poised, motionless, then soared downward to hit the water at last. Hit it with the finality and majesty of death.

SOBs®
SOLDIERS OF BARRABAS

SOBs®
SOLDIERS OF BARRABAS

PACIFIC PAYLOAD

JACK HILD

A GOLD EAGLE BOOK FROM
WORLDWIDE®

TORONTO · NEW YORK · LONDON · PARIS
AMSTERDAM · STOCKHOLM · HAMBURG
ATHENS · MILAN · TOKYO · SYDNEY

First edition March 1988

ISBN 0-373-61623-6

Special thanks and acknowledgment to
John Preston for his contribution to this work.

Printed in Canada

1

"I actually believe that my life is complete now, Linda." Ronald Hamilton took his wife's hand and held it tightly as the two of them looked out their hotel room window.

Linda Hamilton knew that she wasn't seeing the place the way her husband was. She also knew it wasn't the time to intrude on his memories and his thoughts.

"All those years at home, I just wanted to come back here one more time and see it."

Linda listened to Ron speak, but as she looked out over the azure blue of the Matali harbor, she simply couldn't see anything but the tropical paradise that was spread before them as they stood on the balcony of their suite in the Royal Hotel.

But Ron had seen Matali at a different time and in a different way. The place held many of his memories of the Second World War. He had been brought to Matali after he'd been wounded in battle and, near death, almost abandoned on the beaches of Saipan. The spot where he'd been nursed back to health also saw his departure when he'd been sent back to the United States.

Everything had changed in the years since he'd first met Linda, not long before he'd been shipped to the Pacific by the Marines. They had been so young then; and now they were well over sixty. They had survived the war and gone on with their lives, raising their four children—all of them now adults—and being happy with their peaceful lives in Michigan.

Matali was, Linda knew, the place where Ron felt everything had been made possible. There were so many different important decisions that altered people's lives, she mused, but a man would pick out one that had to do with war as the most significant one in his own history.

She didn't begrudge him that, not at all. She was glad they were able to come back to the island and look out over the beauty of it. It must reinforce Ron's dreams, she thought to herself, to see it appear so beautiful.

She shuddered a bit when she remembered the way his thoughts about this place had been transformed. He misunderstood and supposed that the breeze that had just then picked up from the ocean had chilled her. He released her hand and put an arm around her shoulder to warm her.

But mere arms couldn't erase the pictures that had flooded her mind, the way her husband acted when he'd come back from the war. They had gotten married just before he'd gone overseas, the way so many young people had done. When Ron returned stateside, she had had an apartment waiting for them in their old hometown outside of Lansing. He moved right in, a man who now should live with his wife, not a boy going to his mother's side.

Those first many months, he woke up screaming almost every night. His mind was plagued with the horrid memories of war, of those things that men experience and that women so seldom know anything about.

At first, Ron would never tell her anything about what he'd seen in battle. He wouldn't describe for her the images of hell on earth that invaded his mind at night and caused him such torment. Eventually, though, some of it came out: the bodies they'd stumble over that had so quickly decomposed in the tropical heat, the bloated bellies that broke open as soon as they were touched, sending a stench of human death into the air and overpowering the scent of the ever-blossoming orchids growing wild in the jungles of the Pacific.

Or he'd be standing nonchalantly next to a friend, someone Ron had shared a beer with the night before while they'd talked about their girls back home, only to have an unexpected and unannounced round of artillery fire send a wave of shrapnel through the air. The man's head was blown away so suddenly that the mindless torso stayed upright for a moment before it crumpled lifeless to the ground.

Those were the demons her husband had to learn to cope with when he arrived back in the United States and understood that there would never be an easy life after that, not ever.

When their oldest son, James, went to Vietnam, Ron spent the entire time the boy was overseas reliving his personal terrors and horrors. "He'll need someone when he comes back," Ron told his wife.

She was to have her own torments, of course, but when their son did return, with one leg missing, Ron took James, and they went off to the primitive camp the family kept for vacations on the Upper Peninsula. James had changed when they came back. Nothing could heal his body, but his father had helped heal his soul.

What did men talk about when they were alone? Women have always wondered about that. Linda knew what that one conversation had been, at least, and she hated the fact that it had had to happen. Men talk about war—she understood that—and it had been time for the father to tell the son how to live with the memory of battles, victories and defeats.

It was so different, the way men and women dealt with these things. A woman would nurture and protect, allowing her maternal instincts to take over. A man's way was to cauterize, killing off lingering pain and limiting damage with quick, hard action.

Ron himself had learned that lesson well, Linda knew. He'd done what men must have been doing since time immemorial. He forgot those stories she'd heard when he'd first come home. Soon others took their place.

He romanticized his experience, forgetting as soon as he possibly could the nightmares that brought him awake with cries and sobs. Instead of all the death he'd witnessed, he had begun, years ago, to focus on Matali, the place where his life had been given back by doctors and nurses.

He never talked to the boys or to anyone else about his own heroism or about what he'd done to survive the war. He'd only talk about Matali and the way the sharp-tongued staff at the military hospital had kept the rambunctious young serviceman in line. This was the place where he'd been given his life back. He never talked about those other places where he'd saved his own and other men's lives with his valor and the courage that kept him going twenty-four hours a day as they fought merciless battles with the Japanese enemy.

Linda knew that those memories weren't important to her husband. She leaned against Ron's still-strong chest and nuzzled him a little bit. She smiled to herself, thinking back to her own horror when Ron had gone out and bought a Japanese car.

"How could you!" she'd yelled at him. He'd stared at her blankly, unwilling or unable to make any connection between the Toyota and the enemy that had stalked him in the jungle for so many months.

And the desire to come back to Matali had evolved to become, at some point, the dream of their lives—of Ron's life. He'd started talking about it perhaps ten years previously. He wanted to see the place he'd been reborn, the place where his real life had actually begun.

Because that was the way he remembered it. It all dated from there, the substance of their marriage, the boys borne by her body, the outcome of the love the man and woman had shared, and the good life they had learned to live, without nightmares, without horror.

"I have to see the real place," Ron said. His voice had changed, acquiring an adamant tone she seldom heard.

"But, darling, they told us the other island was off limits. It must be contaminated. Perhaps they used it for nuclear tests or something...."

"No, no," he said, brusquely dismissing his wife's rational explanation. "It was much too close to the population here for that to ever have happened. They're just giving us some runaround.

"Hell, Linda, you and I are good enough sailors that we can just take a boat over there tomorrow. It's less than fifteen nautical miles from here. To be so close and not see it just isn't right."

Linda wouldn't argue any more. She knew that when Ron was in a mood like that it wouldn't do any good. They had learned to be quite good sailors on Lakes Michigan and Superior, and she wasn't at all frightened about going out onto the ocean. She wouldn't try to dissuade Ron; they'd come this far, and it would be a crime to deprive him of the final experience he so badly wanted.

"It's about time we went down for dinner, dear," she said.

He gripped her shoulders more tightly in a heartfelt hug. "Let's go and see what the chef's come up with tonight. I'm sure it's not going to be the shit-on-a-shingle that the hospital fed us all the time when we were here."

That was how he handled everything about the trip: all aspects of their adventure had to be compared to the war experience. The food in the hotel seemed to be a way for him to negate the thought of the horrible food they'd been given in the hospital; the free-flowing cocktails were a means to erase the memories of the dry months he'd spent recuperating. The process was the one they used—both of them—to forget the poverty they'd suffered before Ron had gotten his big breaks in business. The expensive vacations they went on now, like the current one, made up for the deprivations of their early married life, when even an overnight trip to visit his parents had been something to be discussed at great length to determine whether they could really afford the cost of ten gallons of gasoline.

They walked down the stairs of the hotel and went directly into the dining room. "Mr. and Mrs. Hamilton!" Somatu, the young native maître d', greeted them by name. "Your table is waiting for you." He showed them to a booth in the corner that they'd admired the first night they'd arrived. He hadn't forgotten them, and they were pleased with the careful service.

Linda knew that Somatu was responding to the special attention Ron had given the young man. It seemed that some of the natives had been employed in the military hospital where he'd been treated. They were, Ron had told her, especially gentle men, a strange contrast to the fighting men he'd known before he'd gotten to Matali.

The place was alive for Ron; he kept remembering old friends by discovering their features in the faces of strangers, and it was clear to her that he often wondered if someone like Somatu could be the son or grandson of an orderly who had worked in the medical camp attached to the hospital. If they were, then Ron had a special sense of obligation to them. He'd gone out of his way to be kind and generous with Somatu for that reason—she was sure of it.

There were many others in the room, most of them Americans on vacation, just as they were. Linda ignored them, thankful she and Ron hadn't taken a tour. They had traveled with groups before and enjoyed the way a group could make a lengthy excursion more fun, but the present experience was too private to be shared with anyone else.

Linda looked up from her menu and saw four uniformed men approach Somatu at the doorway of the dining room. "Ron," she said quietly, and then nodded to direct his attention to the scene.

The four men were members of the constabulary of Matali. The guidebooks had stated that the functions of the police and the army were united in one organization in the republic. The men seemed to intimidate Somatu; he looked frightened. He was shaking his head vigorously, giving a negative answer to some question they were asking him.

When the men left, apparently satisfied with whatever they'd heard from the maître d', the young man seemed astonishingly relieved. He began to move around the room, checking on the guests and refilling their water glasses from a pitcher he'd picked up at the busboy's station.

"Problem, Somatu?" Ron asked when the dining room manager got to their own table.

"Nothing, nothing at all, Mr. Hamilton." Somatu had regained his air of self-confidence and joviality.

"Sometimes men in uniforms simply enjoy throwing their weight around. That's all there is to it."

"There was something in the Asian edition of the *Wall Street Journal* that we read on the plane coming over here, something about political trouble here in Matali. Does this have something to do with what's going on?"

"No. Not really. These men, they work for the big-time General Falanu, the head of the constabulary. He would like to turn the republic into his own little kingdom, but he'll never do it. We have to put up with some of his goons, but really, they're no problem.

"The priests rule Matali, Mr. Hamilton. They are the ones who lead our destiny." Somatu seemed to stand slightly taller and with more pride; the priests obviously had his allegiance. "They've proven themselves over the years.

"When you Americans left—" Somatu broke into a big grin to cut any possible misinterpretation of what he was about to say "—the priests, they showed themselves and their power. They were so polite to the U.S. authorities as they took down the flags and closed up shop, and then, as soon as they were gone, the priests rounded up the missionaries and shipped them home, as well." Somatu laughed in spite of himself.

"No offense, if you are believing Christians, but that is not the religion of Matali or our people. We played along with the missionaries while we had to, but it was always the native priests who had charge of our lives, deep inside. They took over then, and they've never let go.

"The priests don't like to deal with foreign governments, and they think the military stuff is silly, irrelevant to the souls, at least the way they see it now. They believe in warriors—don't doubt that for a minute—but big rifles and warships aren't in their minds.

"So they let General Falanu play his diplomatic games and sell his vote in the United Nations and such; they don't care about that. But if they wanted to get rid of him..."

The way that Somatu's eyes sparkled showed his faith in the power of this religious caste.

"I remember them," Ron said dreamily, "from the hospital. They were the only inhabitants of the island in those days. They had some kind of temple out there, and they lived in huts around it, as though it were some kind of big monastery. They hired on as orderlies, and a couple were even nurses, and they would always get into trouble because they would pray over the wounded—not Christian prayers, either."

"Sure," Somatu said, "they thought you were great warriors, you Americans. You were saving Matali from the Japanese, whom they hated and considered true heathens and barbarians. In the legends, great warriors have always appeared in a time of crisis to protect the priests of Matali. They thought you Americans were like that, and used all their powers to help you if they thought you needed them. But they don't live on that island anymore. That was just about the only thing they lost to Falanu; he made them leave when—"

Somatu changed the subject suddenly and skillfully. "Well, that's all in the past, and it's foolish local history you don't need to worry about. Enjoy your dinner.''

After he made some pointed suggestions about dinner choices, Somatu walked away and left the Hamiltons to order their meal from the waiter who appeared as soon as he'd snapped his fingers.

''Do you think this trouble between the priests and the police has something to do with the reason they don't let us on the other islands?''

''Maybe,'' Ron answered Linda's question. ''I can't see why, though. The out islands are utterly barren. The one where they built the hospital was pure volcanic rock. The Seabees were able to get an airstrip built there with dynamite, and it was so isolated it was perfect for the Army's use during the war. But nothing other than a few hardy weeds could survive on the place, believe me.

''That's why I'm so convinced it's not chemicals or anything really dangerous that's making them difficult about our making this visit, Linda. It would have cost a fortune to blast into the rock and store anything.

''No, I think Somatu's just explained the reason for all this red tape we've run up against: the general's boys are just being bullies. I saw lots of it in the war. Put an MP uniform on someone, or else give some twenty-year-old jerk with a ROTC degree an officer's commission, and they have to prove their authority.

''This has made up my mind, sweetheart. Tomorrow, we're going to rent that boat from the old man Somatu recommended, and we're going to go out there ourselves. The charts are clear and up-to-date, and there's just no reason for us to not make this final part of the journey.''

Linda knew better than to argue at that point. The waiter arrived with the first course, and they began to eat. The decision was made.

THEY RENTED THE YACHT the next day. When they were younger and the boys had been around for the summer, Linda and Ron had sailed. But in their later years, when there wasn't a willing and enthusiastic crew around, they'd turned in their sailboat for a Boston Whaler motor launch, not unlike the one they had just rented.

"Now, you sure you don't want to hire a crew?" Mr. Samsuna asked carefully. "I got good boys who be glad to wait on you hand and foot."

"No, no," Ron answered with his usual good-natured smile. "This is just fine, thanks. We're pretty good at this. We've had lots of practice."

The other man shrugged. He obviously thought that crewing for yourself wasn't the proper way for an American couple to spend their retirement. But it was a decent boat, and the rental for two days' use was found money for the man. It wasn't going out on a long-term charter right now, and it wouldn't have done him any good sitting in the harbor at Matali.

Ron was a competent, careful boatman. Linda noticed that Mr. Samsuna was visibly relieved after he'd watched the way Ron maneuvered the vessel out of its slip and then into the blue waters of the port.

Ron didn't really pick up any speed until they were well away from the dock, as though he understood that Samsuna was judging him. Then, as the boat passed the arcing arms of Matali Harbor and headed into the open waters of the Pacific, he opened the throttle more. The nose of the boat, powered by the surge of energy generated by the twin Chrysler engines, lifted up at first; then the hull settled down to parallel the surface of the deep waters.

Linda sat on the deck, her scarf whipped by the warm tropical wind, and watched the beauty of Matali disappear behind them. They were supposedly just going around the island, taking an extra day and a night to explore the wilder part of the land on the other side. But they weren't headed in that direction. Ron was going straight toward the Rock, as he called it.

Linda had seen the real name for the place on the map: Devil's Land. She wondered what strange native legend had lent its name to the evidently uninhabited volcanic remnant.

She was surprisingly at peace with herself and the trip. It made her feel wonderful to know that Ron was exorcising his last ghost. He was the one who had said it: his life was complete now.

IT DIDN'T TAKE LONG before the Rock came into view. It was a striking vision when it began to rise up over the horizon. Linda went up to the wheel to join Ron and to stand beside him.

"It's so strange, so weirdly beautiful," she said to him, shouting to be heard over the wind and the roar of the boat's engines, though her emotions were such that she'd have whispered if she could have.

The Rock was composed of a seemingly unbroken piece of black ore. It rose suddenly out of the sea like the Rock of Gibraltar. The tip had come into view first, and as they approached it, it seemed that there was more and more bulk constantly being exposed.

"The airstrip was right in the middle of that thing," Ron said to her.

"How could they have built it there?" Linda asked.

"There's a plateau. The formation was so flat at that one place that it really didn't take much to get a good long strip of land on it. Then there's a freshwater spring in the middle of the plateau, and then, on the other side of the island, it cascades to earth like a waterfall in the Rockies or something. It's very beautiful; I'll show it to you later.

"The waterfall's end is the only part of the place that's not volcanic rock, with a beach that's sandy but made of the same material so the sand has the same black color. On this side, where we're going in, there's a small inlet. It's where the hospital ships used to bring in the men."

"If this place is so perfectly situated, why isn't it settled like Matali?" Linda asked.

"There's water, but not enough soil to support much vegetation, and so there's no game. There's nothing here to sustain human life, just beauty and a location that was great during the war. This was perfect for medical purposes then, when they wanted to have Matali for other military uses. That airfield on the main island—the one where our jet landed—was a major refueling point for our bombers as they were being transported to the Orient. The main island was inundated with soldiers and sailors on R and R or in transit for one reason or another.

"This place was silent; the medical planes could come and go and not worry about military priorities. Everything was easily brought in by sea or air for the patients and the staff. The Rock was just one big hospital. Now it's gone back to its original state.

"I wonder what buildings are still left...."

Even with all the other noises, Linda could hear the wistful tone in Ron's voice. He sounded as though he were going back to check out his old Boy Scout camp, not the hospital where he had nearly died and where he'd suffered so much pain.

Only now could Linda see the full outline of the island, where the ocean crashed against the rocks at its base. They were coming close to it, and she could see its entire enormity. There wasn't one peak, as she'd thought from a distance, but many, and they ringed the island. There was a depression in the center of them. Ron pulled in the throttle, and the boat's engines lowered to a purr as he carefully studied the charts to make sure there weren't any navigational hazards.

Then he headed into the small harbor. Linda had gone back down onto the main deck of the boat to watch the approach. She was near the prow when she saw it all. She knew immediately that they were in trouble.

Almost as though someone had read her mind, two enormous sleek speedboats came rushing toward them. They were painted black, the hulls so smooth she thought it must be specially treated plastic. She was close to guessing right. She was looking at the epoxy surface of two Formula Ones, cigar boats, power-hungry craft with twin engines twice the size of their own Boston Whaler's, propelling aerodynamically designed craft only a fraction of the size of their rented yacht.

The boats speeded toward them. Ron barely had time to react, and even then there was clearly nothing he could do. The two interceptors circled them and blocked their exit to the ocean.

Linda looked at her husband with a worried expression, but he could only shrug. They had been told over and over again that the Rock was abandoned.

While their attention was held by the two boats, their own craft moved just far enough into the inlet to reveal, when she turned toward land again, something even more astonishing.

Rising up from the black volcanic mass was a scene out of a science-fiction movie. She saw enormously tall towers constructed from metal beams, and in the middle of one was what she took to be a rocket, just like those she was used to seeing on the television news. It was mammoth, beyond her ability to gauge its size.

She quickly realized that she could see the structure only because they were inside the harbor. From out at sea, it would have been obstructed by the black peaks of the island.

The boats were alongside now, and from each one ropes were thrown to tie the speed launches to their yacht. The three-man crews were all standing on the decks with large, mean-looking rifles in their hands. Linda instinctively grabbed Ron's arm, all at once realizing how much she'd always looked to him for protection.

The crewmen were all dressed in white tropical uniforms of a sort. They wore tight, clinging T-shirts and shorts that left their tanned legs bare. The almost innocent-looking outfits were in contrast to the severe looks on their faces as they studied the Hamiltons.

One man seemed to be in charge, though he was dressed the same way as the rest of them and didn't appear noticeably older. He shouted an order in some language Linda couldn't understand, and the others jumped to obey.

They boarded the boat and rushed at the couple. There was nothing Ron and Linda could do but follow passively as they were led off the yacht. One of the boarding party stayed behind and took the charter's controls.

"We're American citizens!" Ron complained even as he stepped over onto one of the cigar boats. Even if he was smart enough not to try to fight the younger men, he wasn't going to submit without some kind of protest.

"I demand to see our ambassador! You'll turn this into an international incident, and I warn you I have influence back in my country."

No one paid any attention to him.

THE ENTIRE CHAPTER became even more surreal once they were on land. The young soldiers hadn't even acknowledged Ron's constant protests, which he'd escalated in sharpness of tone and frequency. Linda recognized his frustrated reaction and knew better than to say anything to him.

On the island they were taken up a steep embankment toward the plateau on which Ron's hospital had once stood and where, just minutes ago, Linda had seen the missile launching pad. The pad was invisible as they ascended the side of the island slope in an ultramodern elevator. Then, when they reached the apex, the space-age structure with its missile encapsulated inside it was again visible.

There was a group of men waiting at the top of the plateau. The guards from the boats simply left them standing there and immediately and silently returned to the elevator cages and began to descend, going back to the boats.

"*Spies!*" one of the new group confronting them spit out. "The CIA, I'm sure of it, Gasteau! I warned you that the Americans would come here and invade us and..."

"Shut up." The man who spoke, the one who was evidently called Gasteau, stared at Ron and Linda intently. He was obviously in charge. Linda looked back at him and was even more puzzled. He appeared to be their own age, a little over sixty. He was smoking a cigarette stuck into a long holder, something that seemed oddly anachronistic in the modern-age setting.

"We're not CIA," Ron insisted. "We're just tourists. I was here, during the Second World War, at a hospital on this island. I just wanted to see what it was like now. I just wanted to return to see what had happened to the place."

"Ah, yes—" Gasteau smiled in a way that made Linda think of a kindly old professor "—you Americans are always attempting to find your roots, aren't you?"

He let the smile evaporate and went back to studying them. There were more of the white-uniformed guards standing around him, and another older man who, like Gasteau, wore a white laboratory coat over his civilian attire.

Gasteau took a long drag on his cigarette. "I believe them," he said, and his voice had the authority of a pronouncement.

Linda sighed with enormous relief, but it was Ron who responded. "We just want to go back to our hotel on Matali," he said, the fight gone from his voice. "We're sorry if we've intruded...."

"Yes, unfortunately you have," Gasteau said, his voice betraying a bit of annoyance. "And even if you are not the CIA, you cannot leave."

Linda couldn't imagine what he meant. His quiet demeanor had lulled her into thinking that the man was simply some kindly old teacher. She didn't even register danger when he reached over and unholstered a Beretta 9 mm from the belt of one of the guards. The younger man didn't move, either; there wasn't even a hint that he found Gasteau's move strange in the least.

Gasteau pointed the pistol at Ron, who seemed stunned, frozen in place. Linda heard the shot before she even understood it was going to happen. She jumped back a single step, reacting involuntarily to the loud noise.

She turned and saw Ron sprawled on his back on the ground. She saw the tiny hole in his forehead where the bullet had entered his skull, just above his eyes. She didn't even scream, too entranced by the sight of how tiny the mortal wound was. To think that such a small thing could take a human life.

Then Ron's head turned, falling to the side from nothing more than gravity, because only physical laws were determining his movement now. There was no life in him to allow him to make those decisions for himself. She could see the exit wound now. It was so much bigger than the one in front. Out of it oozed a slow stream of red blood, much redder than she'd expected it to be. There was also a small flow of gray matter—his brains, she realized.

She turned to look at Gasteau. This, she now thought with understanding is what men know about and what they talk about when they come back from war. They talk about the intolerable fragility of human existence; they describe how someone you love can stand beside you laughing at one moment and then, in the next instant, be gone. This was just what Ron's nightmares had been about when he'd come back to Michigan and slept in her bed with her.

She studied Gasteau and realized that she was going to die. She looked down as the barrel of the Italian automatic was aimed again, this time at her. He must be a good shot, she thought to herself. She never had a chance to think about what a foolish last thought that was.

It seemed to her that she saw the bullet. She saw the explosion that erupted out of the end of the barrel. She even thought she saw the small projectile of metal as it hurtled toward her, aimed right between her eyes.

She never did hear it, though. The message of the sound of the explosion didn't make it to her brain as quickly as the sight had done. By the time it might have registered, it was too late. She was dead on the volcanic rock surface, her dead arms wrapped around her husband's cadaver.

"TAKE THEM AWAY," Gasteau said calmly as he handed the pistol back to the guard.

"I told you, damn it, the Americans—"

"They are no problem," Gasteau cut off Knudsen's whine. He turned to the guard and continued with his orders. "Put their bodies back on the boat and make it appear like an accident—the coral reefs on the north side of Matali would do. Leave their corpses there. The sharks will surely dispose of them. No one will be suspicious at all."

The guard put the gun back in its holster, snapped the holster shut and then saluted. He shouted orders to the men around them, and they quickly came to action, groups of four of them each taking hold of the lifeless limbs of the dead Hamiltons and taking them down the stairway toward the shoreline.

"Gasteau . . ." Knudsen tried once more, obviously anxious to worry some more.

The scientist couldn't be bothered. "It's finished, done with. Now let's go back to our scheduling problem, if you don't mind. We have important work to do."

2

Miss Roseline had seldom seen the senator seem so happy. The old man was in his wheelchair, as always. The motorized chair was something his secretary thought should be labeled a dangerous weapon. The joystick made it easy for the ancient legislator to race around the ground floor of his Georgetown mansion, caroming to and fro and knocking at least one piece of furniture and one member of his staff to the floor every day.

She kept her peace about the chair, though, as she did about almost everything that went on in the huge showplace in the most exclusive district of the capital. Discretion was something for which confidential secretaries were paid extremely well those days. The scandals that had rocked both the administration and the opposition candidates for the President's office in the next election had increased those salaries even more.

Acting like some other officeholders in Washington, the senator had taken only a little time to think after the latest flurry of activity in the capital to determine that the quite lovely and intelligent Miss Roseline deserved a pay raise. Anyone who was so necessary for his functioning needed to be well taken care of; that was obvious.

Miss Roseline was even willing to assume the menial duties of a waitress under the circumstances. The senator obviously would rather not have any of his domestic staff walking in and out of a meeting like the current confab. Recently arrived immigrants weren't the kind of people who would be welcome to overhear discussions between members of the United States Congress, the National Aeronautics and Space Administration—commonly called NASA—and the Air Force.

It wasn't just the company that had put the senator in such a good mood, of course. He was such a mean-spirited person that pleasant comradeship would never do that, Miss Roseline realized as she bent down and offered the senator his bourbon and water. The old man didn't even deign to acknowledge her as he grabbed the glass.

She moved to General Masterson, who was more polite, smiling at her as he took his Scotch.

Miss Roseline was careful not to block anybody's view of the television screen as she went over to serve Admiral Powelton his rye and ginger ale. After all, the show they were watching was the real reason for the senator's great joy.

She continued around the room, carefully remembering who of the military officers' staff had what to drink. Then she went and stood by the wall, near the doorway, waiting for whatever else the senator might want from her.

To pass the time, she joyfully calculated the hourly rate of pay her new salary meant. At the number of dollars she was being paid, she'd gladly stand there and look like an old-fashioned woman for him. She had mortgage payments to make on the retirement home in Arkansas, after all, and a condominium in the Watergate had an inflated maintenance fee, as well. Though she didn't mind that, since the value of her apartment had inflated even more in the years she'd owned it.

Then there was the new Mercedes she was thinking of buying to replace her BMW. A woman her age couldn't afford to look unsuccessful in a city like Washington. Ah, well, she thought, it was of no concern. With her new salary, she'd be able to pay for the new automobile in cash.

Now, she realized, if there was a nice *big* scandal in the administration again soon, especially one involving a secretary's leaking of information to an independent prosecutor or, even better, to the *Washington Post*, she might consider a cottage at Rehobeth Beach, the oceanside resort that was attracting more and more Washingtonians during the summer. That was the best place—bar none—for a woman in her position to attract a very wealthy and powerful husband.

The senator was definitely out of the running. It wasn't just that his wounds had left him incapacitated below the waist—though that was certainly a matter of some concern for a woman with Miss Roseline's healthy appetites. He was simply so old that he had no future. She wanted the excitement of a man who was going places. In her daydreams, Miss Roseline, like every other attractive woman in the District, pictured herself as another Jackie Kennedy, standing beside the new Jack as they blasted their way along the campaign trail.

But if he had been younger, the senator would have done nicely. Miss Roseline knew things about the senator's past and present that she was sure the others in the room would love to hear more about. The senator was the subject of constant gossip in the city that thrived on information.

Was he really connected with the upper echelons of American industry? That was one rumor, that he was the spokesman for the biggest of American big business. He certainly had access to tremendous amounts of money, more than he ever admitted having in his own considerable bank accounts. Of course, the rest of the rumors said that the source of money was criminal.

There was, according to some wags about town, a special tax that the underworld imposed upon itself, a secret account that was administered by the senator to make sure that everything that needed to happen to assure America's place in the world was accessible to those who could provide the means to accomplish it.

Miss Roseline smiled to herself. There were so many rumors, but really, very few people understood just what the senator was all about. And she was one of them.

The men's conversation was suddenly stifled. Only the senator called out, "Here we go!" He tried to shriek like a small boy, but his old voice cracked, and the sound was more like a slight obscenity.

On the television screen was a large rocket. Miss Roseline knew almost as much about it as the men did; it was part of her job to understand these things.

The rocket was a Titan missile, the largest in the American arsenal. Originally developed to deliver long-range nuclear weapons, the Titan was now the great American hope for outer space. As Miss Roseline was only too aware, the men in the room were horribly chagrined by that fact. The Titan was, to their way of thinking, old-fashioned. They hated being tied to what they considered outdated technology. At least the damned thing worked, though. Or at least it did sometimes.

There was a huge plume of fire and smoke at the rocket's base. The machine seemed to almost shudder as it was slowly lifted off the ground by the explosion. Then it began to gain more and more speed.

"Go, go baby, go!" General Masterson screamed with all the vigor he had used as a quarterback of the Air Force Academy football team at Colorado Springs.

"Yes, yes." Admiral Powelton was quieter but just as anxious as he watched the big missile start to speed through the air. "Oh, please, God . . ."

The group was transfixed by the spectacle. The picture was a special transmission from Vandenburg Air Force Base in California. The general public was getting a much more distant view of the same launch effort.

The American space program was in disarray. The shuttle disaster had forced a yearlong delay in an essential part of the defense work that had to be done if the President's plans for an all-encompassing space defense system were going to be realized.

The mainstay of the program had become the unmanned Titan missiles. The expectation was that they had to deliver new satellites into space now. There had been unbelievable disasters in the Titan program in the past few tries. Hundreds of millions of dollars' worth of equipment and even more precious time had been lost.

But if this one missile could make it...

That was the one thing on the mind of every male in the room. For each one there was a different set of priorities, but they all shared the one consuming prayer for the missile's success.

They saw the big bird soaring upward on a perfect path, heading for space. "It's so goddamned beautiful," Masterson said in his loud, cheerful voice.

As though he'd damned the thing, the missile suddenly began to wobble, almost imperceptibly at first. It seemed to be ever so slightly off balance, and only trained people—like the room's occupants—could see it at first. The public wouldn't have discerned what was happening.

There was a collective intake of breath when they saw what was going on. Then the Titan began to spiral more noticeably. "Oh, no, oh, damn..." Powelton couldn't contain himself.

The senator hit a button on his remote control, and the voice of the announcer in the command post of Vandenburg came out over the air.

In steely, unemotional terms, he ordered, "Abort mission."

It was just that easy. None of them had to be told any more, and the senator viciously stabbed the remote control once again. The missile was dangerously close to metropolitan Los Angeles, and if it wasn't blown up into harmless little pieces, it could crash on heavily populated areas and kill countless civilians.

Like a huge Fourth of July firecracker, the missile suddenly disintegrated on the television screen. It turned into a cloud of smoke.

It took a few minutes for the men to react. One of General Masterson's aides dared to speak up. "That kills the civilian program. We don't have any room on any of the remaining missiles for private enterprise satellites."

They all knew what that meant. First, the communications corporations wouldn't have space on American missiles. Each of the corporations had been ready to pay a fortune to get a piece of the sky for the sake of future economic benefits obtained by having their own satellites. The fees could have significantly subsidized the American space program at a time when Congress wasn't inclined to hand out money as it had been in the days of constant success.

Worse, or at least just as bad, it meant that American business would go to other countries. Even the Chinese Communists were rumored to be ready to deal with corporations who were desperate enough to do business with them. The Chinese had the oldest and least sophisticated rockets that were actually capable of getting a payload into orbit, but at least the damn things worked!

So did the senator's wheelchair. The motor came to life as the man began to speed in a larger circle around the chairs where his guests sat. Though unable to walk, the senator hadn't been able to give up some semblance of the pacing that had always been his way of reacting to pressure and tension.

"What kinds of fools do you have in NASA and the Air Force that this kind of thing happens over and over again?!? You *fools*!" None of the assembly dared to say anything to the old man. They were too clearly chagrined.

The chair didn't hesitate; it kept circling the gathering, actually picking up speed.

"What the hell are we going to do? The President's so involved with his internal scandals that we can hardly get his attention about these important matters as it is. Now it'll just seem like one more headache to him.

"The damned international corporations don't have any sense of obligation to this country anymore. They're going to be happy to take their business to Beijing or to the French or anyone else who can deliver for them.

"And you bozos obviously can't do that!"

The large men in their sharply creased uniforms all hung their heads, acting like little boys being chastised in a classroom rather than the leaders of the largest military-scientific complex in the history of the world.

The senator continued his rampage. "The Russians have a shuttle capability now. They have rockets that are years ahead of ours. The Europeans have that damned consortium that can launch private satellites...."

"And the new one," some voice in the background muttered.

Miss Roseline looked quickly to identify the person who had spoken, but none of the junior members of the staff were looking up. Whoever it was had realized his mistake and retreated to safer ground quickly.

"What do you mean, 'the new one'?" The senator's always sour-looking face took on an appearance even more malign than usual.

General Masterson coughed theatrically, as though clearing his throat was a way to take the floor. He didn't seem to want to look the senator directly in the eye. "There are new reports of a consortium of European scientists."

"We know about them. They've been launching that damned Ariane missile from their base near Dakar, in western Africa. They'd already underbid the United States for private missiles for years, depriving us of the potential profit we could have used to get around the shortsighted idiots in Congress."

"No, sir. This is another group, one that seems to be banking on a great deal of secrecy. They've built a base in Matali, in the Pacific—"

"But that's an American territory!" The senator's blood pressure was building again.

"Sir, you sponsored the bill to grant Matali independence five years ago," Miss Roseline said. She was enjoying herself a little too much and bit the inside of her cheek to stop the smile that was creeping across her mouth.

"I did not!" The old man looked as though he might have a stroke.

Miss Roseline—always one to know when to make a placating gesture—crossed to his wheelchair with the bourbon bottle in hand to refill his glass. She only nodded once, forcing a smile this time, to let him know that he had, indeed, put his name on what had once been an inconsequential piece of legislation.

"But, anyway, they're on our side. They wouldn't be aiding and abetting people—"

"Do remember, Senator," Miss Roseline said in a calm voice, "that the world views the European nations as our allies. Why should the Matali government think otherwise? They have no reason to suspect any Europeans as working against us. In any event, the current government is barely in control. It's moving slowly toward a military dictatorship, but there's a strong caste of priests who have the allegiance of the population and keep the officials in check.

"The military head of state—a General Falanu—has been trying for years to break their hold, but he hasn't been able to do it. His only hope has been to increase the power of his armed forces, which costs great amounts of money to maintain, and to subsidize the economy and artificial standards of living, and the result is that he's in constant threat of bankruptcy. He continues to do so, however, in hopes that the financial rewards of his regime will eventually convince his countrymen that his is a better way than the priests'.

"But his program calls for an enormous budget. The rents he's probably getting from the secret European space program would be essential for his success.''

"How do you know all this?'' It was clear to everyone who heard the senator's cry that he wasn't just responding to that one succinct briefing from his secretary. He had obviously gone through the process with her on many different subjects. He wasn't taken aback by that one recitation; he was expressing his accumulated shock at having been caught by her many times before.

Miss Roseline simply smiled enigmatically and stepped back to replace the bourbon bottle on its shelf.

The men ignored the secretary's performance. Admiral Powelton picked up the conversation. "We simply cannot allow any other consortium to gain ground on us. The commercial subsidies we receive from the space program are increasingly essential for our ongoing budgetary needs.''

"Who makes up this new group?'' the senator asked.

"That's the strange part; no one really knows. The other group—the one doing the rockets from Dakar—is government sponsored, and the French are in the lead there. Along with the Germans, the Spanish and the English, they underwrite the Airbus program of civilian jetliners. They make it look very peaceful, but we know that they don't really trust us to stand by them all the time, and the Airbus technology can be shifted over to military use at any time.

"But this new group seems to be made up of some shady types. No allied government appears to be involved. We suspect—but we can't be sure—that some of the European defense contractors who are least tied to the NATO defense alliance have gotten together and built up this shadow corporation, using the regular fronts of Swiss bank accounts, and so on.''

''How do we stop it?'' The senator put the question to the gathering bluntly.

The rest of the men in the room all seemed to shift in their chairs. The answers weren't very comfortable ones.

''We could use moral suasion to have the Matali government close down their operations.''

''We could confront the European governments with our information and ask them just what this consortium is up to.''

The men were well trained to come up only with the most legal of legal alternatives these days. The televised images of hearings on Capitol Hill were emblazoned on their brains. Just the idea of suggesting a covert operation in front of witnesses was too terrifying for any of them to even consider it.

''Oh, get out of here!'' the senator suddenly screamed. ''All of you. *Out!''*

One by one, the officers stood and sheepishly left the room, with only the most senior of them daring to offer a hand to the senator. They regretted their decision; the old man sneered at their gestures and waved them off, as he would annoying insects.

When they were alone, Miss Roseline closed the doors of the senator's living room and waited for him to speak. The house staff would gather the others' coats and see them to the front door.

As she had known he would, the senator finally looked at her. "Call him," he spat out at her.

"I already did. His service will be getting ahold of him just about now. I suspect he'll be here within the hour."

The senator punched the arm of his wheelchair in frustration.

WALKER JESSUP STUDIED the enormous hunk of prime beef that was on the plate in front of him. He smiled with all the joy of a Romeo contemplating the favors of his Juliet.

The big sirloin meant as much to him as any woman ever would. His mouth was watering with anticipation of its taste and texture. He held back for a moment. He was in the Palm, justifiably the most famous steak house in the District of Columbia.

There are many fashionable restaurants in Washington, places where the rich and powerful go to see and be seen. Knowing which ones are the latest trend is a science. But just as good steak always has the heart of an American male, while different cuisines come in and out of favor, so the Palm always retains its position near the top of the list of power dining places in Washington.

Jessup wasn't there for the prestige, though. He was there for the meat.

A slight murmur worked its way up from his chest as he contemplated the slab of rare steak. It had just come out of the kitchen, and there was nothing to be lost in enjoying the visual delights for a moment longer. He was doing what another man does when studying the breasts of a beautiful woman before entering her, allowing his physical need to build to a point that made the consummation of passion all the more exquisite.

Jessup picked up his wineglass and took a deep draft of the rare and smooth Margaux he'd ordered as the perfect accompaniment to the meal. He closed his eyes for a moment of sheer hedonistic delight.

Putting down the glass, he picked up his knife and fork, ready to begin his act of love.

A sudden flurry of faint but insistent beep-beep-beeps made him freeze, his cutlery poised motionlessly above the plate. The moment of bliss was forever lost, and Jessup looked down at the pager in his belt in disbelief at the betrayal just committed.

No one turned to examine the source of the noise interrupting the subdued chatter in the dining room. Being paged was a social status game, and there were many who would have arranged to be called while they dined at the Palm, just for the sake of underlining their importance.

Jessup automatically reached down and pushed the button on the pager. His work was too important to have a voice message conveyed. Instead, the machine, half the size of a cigarette package, contained a miniature dot-matrix printer. With only a slight whistling sound, a piece of printed paper was spewed out.

Jessup looked bitterly at his steak before ne ripped off the paper and brought it up to the tabletop so he could read it.

The encoded message was simple for him to decipher. He was to go to Georgetown, and he was to do it *now*. The call was top priority. A national emergency was in progress. Nothing—not love nor money, not even a perfect steak at the Palm—could justify anything other than an immediate response.

Jessup stood. His huge stomach, which had been longing to enfold the sirloin in its girth, ballooned over the white linen cloth. Its bulk was so great that it almost knocked the plate off the surface—as though it wanted to give the meat one last kiss before departing.

Jessup didn't have time for that now. His standing up had brought the immediate attention of the waiter, who was scurrying over to him as quickly as possible. "Check," Jessup said, biting out the words.

That miserable son of a bitch was going to pay for this one, Jessup swore as he began to follow the waiter to the cashier's desk.

MISS ROSELINE SHOWED JESSUP into the senator's living room. She knew perfectly well who the obese man was. He was whispered about in the corridors of power all over Washington. The Fixer. He had once been in the CIA. He'd also been involved in some National Security Council activities at one point or another. He'd been in and out of nearly every sensitive post in government.

He'd gone free-lance. The senator was his most prized customer, and he was the senator's most prized weapon. There were simply times when the normal channels wouldn't do. It was in the senator's best interests to make sure there was always one arm of power and force available to him—and his allies— when there was no other avenue for action.

The two men went through a charade of pleasantries that fooled neither them nor the politely silent secretary who served coffee and brandy. They loathed each other. And, with an even greater passion, the senator despised the actual men whom Jessup would use to fulfill his orders. He still claimed that the head of Jessup's fighting group, Nile Barrabas, was responsible for his physical disability. On occasion, the senator had experienced mellowed feelings toward these people he relied on, but the resentment for his dependence on them always won out.

"There seems to be a slight problem in the Pacific, Walker," the senator said easily as soon as he could talk without appearing to be anxious.

"It's one of those very delicate situations. It seems there's an international electronics syndicate doing some things that aren't exactly in the best interests of the United States. We were hoping that your people might be able to put a wrench in their progress, slow them down until the U.S. has enough of a lead on them."

"Industrial sabotage?" Jessup was still thinking about that steak. The miserable gnome had taken him away from something that lovely just to talk about a matter any collection of goons from the streets could handle!

"Well, that's such an indelicate way to put it," the senator hedged, trying to deflect the question.

"It's hardly the American way to handle these problems," Jessup said. His years in the CIA had taught him that there were, in fact, many different ways in which a country had to defend itself. No one won wars and battles with self-righteousness; victory came by playing as dirty as the opponent.

"Such a minor event." The senator wasn't going to buy that kind of argument. "Of course, it's in the South Seas. I'm sure your...operatives will enjoy this as a vacation. In fact, I don't think it would be necessary to pay the usual fee, do you? After all, it's—"

"Professionals don't haggle over their prices, Senator." Jessup laid his coffee cup on the bulge of his well-dressed stomach. The suit he was wearing had been tailored by one of the best—and most expensive—shops on Savile Row in London. Only because his meal had been interrupted, the suit was spotless. His enthusiasm for food seldom allowed him to eat gracefully; he was more like a young and passionate lover when he ate, and he didn't worry about the niceties of etiquette when he did it.

He was actually thinking that when he answered the senator. He was pleased that his suit was in such good shape. He was not at all pleased that a gorgeous piece of beef had been left at the altar of the Palm because of the senator's call.

The man would pay for the infidelity he'd made Jessup commit. He'd pay dearly.

"But this would be only a quick journey to the Pacific. It won't even be a dangerous assignment, I should think."

"An ability to face danger isn't the only thing my operation gives you," remarked Jessup, whose business hid behind the innocuous corporate name of International Consultants. "We also provide you with complete secrecy. The one thing you can always count on—you *have* always counted on—is the discretion I provide.

"You don't have many options in this one, Senator. You're going after a private corporation owned by citizens of countries that are supposed to be your allies or neutrals in the cold war. It's not the kind of thing you'd want to have come out in the press or have to explain to your colleagues in Congress, is it?

"But I'll answer for you: no. The fee is the same as always: half a million for each one who goes in."

"Well, this is so simple—" the senator paused in an attempt to appear sly "—perhaps only two or three of them would be necessary."

"You know better than that, Senator. The whole team, always. It's never broken apart."

The senator's face grew even more sour when he realized his money-saving maneuver wasn't going to work.

Jessup wondered if he was pressing the man too hard. In reality, if it hadn't been for that dinner he was missing, he might have been willing to negotiate. It just wasn't the night for it.

"Done."

Jessup studied the senator carefully as the older man sipped at his cognac. The fine brandy didn't bring any pleasure to the senator's face. Perhaps it was just his knowing that he was doing something that involved

Barrabas, whom Jessup knew he hated. Or maybe it was losing in the negotiations; the old man certainly understood the value of a dollar and wouldn't be happy to have lost the chance to save a few million.

Or maybe the whole thing was more involved and more dangerous than he was letting on.

Jessup stood up to leave. He glanced at his watch and grimaced as soon as he did. The Palm had stopped serving by this hour. The best he'd be able to do, because of the time of night, was something quick at one of the nearby Georgetown bistros. What a waste.

The night ended with the two men in equally foul moods.

3

Nile Barrabas was sitting on a beach on the Mediterranean when the call came through.

He was wearing only his swimsuit. His skin had become deeply tanned over the past week while he'd been here with Erika Dykstra. His predominantly white hair was a stark contrast to his body's smooth brownness, broken only by the strangely pale spots where bullets had entered his body. The history of most of those wounds was gone, lost in the present where he insisted on living his life. But the scar tissue that had resulted hadn't the pigmentation to take on new color.

The beach attendant from the hotel brought him the cryptic note: "International delegation needed to deal with Pacific trade."

Erika was used to these interruptions. The beautiful Dutchwoman didn't even have to know the words of the message to understand that her own vacation was ending, and probably right away.

It was something that came from loving a man like Nile. You took him when you could, and you didn't question why he left when he did. She closed her eyes and waited for him to talk.

He crumpled the small piece of paper in his hand. He wondered what he was feeling. He didn't do that often. Introspection wasn't a big thing for him. Action was more like it.

He turned to look at Erika. As soon as he did, and saw the sleek body that was barely covered by her tiny two-piece bikini, he felt a stirring. There were many things that changed, he thought, but this one thing seemed constant. The desire they had for each other was just as fresh, as easily aroused, as it had been in the early days of their affair.

He put a hand on her bare belly. It was slightly rounded, just enough to be feminine, but without a hint of extra flesh. Her skin was warm from the bright sun. He was surprised by how erotic he thought that was.

"Let's go upstairs," he said, almost bluntly.

Erika opened her eyes again when he spoke. She lifted up her sunglasses as though she needed to see him more clearly to discern his meaning. She felt something liquid moving inside her when she did. Without the barrier of the tinted glasses, the quick sunlight showed off the male power of the torso next to her. There was something especially appealing about the rawness of Nile Barrabas.

Let's go upstairs was such a typical thing for him to say. Another man, dealing with a woman of her wealth and the sophistication of her Amsterdam background, would have made it a request, often a plea. Only Barrabas would think of telling her that she was going to have sex, and only Barrabas thought that his desires were enough justification for it to happen right away.

She didn't even answer. She just stood up and began to gather her few things. They could leave their towels where they were. The attendants from the resort would take care of them.

Wearing only their swimwear, they walked up to the hotel. Nile knew that they were being watched. Men and women studied the two of them with varying degrees of envy and lust. They were always the center of attention when they traveled. There was his size. His two-hundred-plus pounds of muscle hugged his six-foot-four frame, and there were those symbols of war that were his scars. Her presence wasn't only physical, though her sensuousness was always there. Besides that, she had a constant air of being a woman in control and of always belonging.

They walked through the lobby of the small and luxurious hotel and up the one set of stairs to the suite they'd rented. The rooms were cooled by a circulating fan; the windows were open. There was air-conditioning, but they were both people who would rather be in a natural atmosphere if they could possibly do it. They would resort to an air conditioner only if it was unbearably hot.

"Shower?" she asked him when he'd closed the door.

He looked at her and shook his head.

She tossed her bag to the side, then took off her sunglasses and threw them on top of it. She reached behind herself and untied the knot. The top of her bikini fell off. He moved forward and took her in his arms, propelled by something unnamed, something even beyond the excitement coiling between them.

There was often a slight pause at the beginning of their lovemaking, as though they were holding back, almost afraid of their own responses.

But he held her tightly now, and she responded uninhibitedly. Even as their mouths covered each other's, she reached down and tugged at the waistband of his swimtrunks. She began at the back, and as soon as the stretchy material was down over the mounds of his buttocks, she grabbed each one with a hand and squeezed hard, pulling him toward her even more emphatically.

He kept his attention on her face, moving his lips more quickly over her cheeks, her chin, her forehead. He was making love to her, wondering at the touch of her beauty and how it could meet and combine with his power and strength in a perfect balance. Her hands moved to the front of his waist and tugged again, stripping off his suit until it dropped to his ankles, leaving him naked, hard and vulnerable.

Her hands explored him shamelessly, knowingly, with the familiarity born of many pairings. Her explorations of him were anything but tentative. They were almost lewd, yet never that.

He couldn't stop now. His body told him—and her—that he wanted her and that he wanted her immediately. He fondled her, and her silken heat and writhing hips told him she was just as anxious.

He carried her to the bed and hovered above her as she lay sprawled out on the cover. They stopped by silent agreement and just looked, staring deeply into each other's eyes. Exchanging silent messages of lust and desire, they saw the other parts of each other that they were less sure of. Somewhere in there was need—not physical need, but emotional need. Neither one of them wanted to explore that. That was their taboo, not the access to each other's body, but the fear that there would be some claim beyond the sexual one.

He put a hand on the side of her head in a delicate gesture, a loving one. He left it there and wondered at how huge his palm seemed to be when put up against her. Her face looked startlingly white against his hand, and so fragile. Her expression didn't change. Not for the first time, he felt suddenly and incredibly sad, because he understood that if they explored their taboo they would both realize he was the one who needed her more and wanted her more.

He could never admit that to her, or to anyone else, but he did do the best he could. He leaned down and very gently placed his lips on hers, hardly even kissing her.

She opened her mouth and bit his lower lip. It was so sudden, so passionate and unexpected, that he nearly yelled out. Then he saw her eyes. They'd changed. There had been desire there before, but now there was a fire in the way they sparkled.

If she'd bitten any harder, he was sure she'd have drawn blood. But that wasn't what she wanted. He shifted his weight, and her thighs opened up to him. They were joined in a long, smooth slide that they never wanted to stop.

As though poised on the brink of a takeoff, he looked at her carefully once more, but now her eyes were closed while her hips surged up to meet him. He wondered if he was the only image she saw behind her eyelids as he began to move in synchrony with her.

And he knew he didn't want to know the answer, not now, nor ever.

"THE SURFMASTER HOTEL. It's on Waikiki. I can get the Concorde from Paris to New York tonight and catch the nonstop from there to Honolulu, with any luck. I can make it in thirty-six hours. Less by the clock; the time change is in my favor."

Barrabas could feel Erika's long fingernails moving up and down his spine on his naked back. She began each motion at his neck and didn't stop until she reached his thighs. She kept it up, repeating the trailing touch countless times.

She was listening—he was sure of it. She'd want the information that he was giving to his team in these international long-distance calls. He hadn't actually told her his plans directly; this was the first time she understood just what they were.

Nile heard Geoff Bishop talk to someone in the background. It would be Lee Hatton, the one woman who was a part of the team. Geoff was the pilot of the group known as the SOBs—the Soldiers of Barrabas, named after their leader, Nile Barrabas.

Bishop had a lodge in the Laurentian Mountains north of Montreal, and Lee Hatton, a medical doctor who came from a long line of military forebears, had her own place, an estate on Majorca. The love affair between the two of them kept them moving back and forth between the continents.

"Lee says she has numbers for Claude in New York and for Nanos in California. We figure Billy Two's with him, or he's left word with him. Liam's in California, too. We'll call them. Want us to call Beck, as well?"

"No. I'll do that myself." Getting ahold of Nate Beck, the computer specialist on the team, was always the easiest assignment. He was perpetually holed up in his oceanside home in Old Lyme, Connecticut. The greatest passion in the man's life was his computers, and they were all set up there.

"Okay, Chief, we're on our way. But nothing special?"

Nile understood Geoff's question. The team wasn't used to simple operations. Their business was usually much more complex than the present assignment seemed to be.

"No," he assured his man, "nothing at all. Just be at the hotel at the rendezvous time."

Nile hung up the phone and rolled over. He pulled Erika into his arms and pressed her body against his. Their sweat was still covering their flesh, something he liked. It made them seem more real, somehow. He reached over and kissed her, and the mingled heat and scent of their bodies teased his nostrils.

She pulled away and stood up to turn, and he got a wonderful view of her backside, which was firm, the skin taut over her curves.

"We'd better shower if you're going to catch that plane," she said. She began moving around the suite, collecting a few things that would help him with his packing. Then she went through a doorway, leaving him alone and naked on the bed. He heard the water start, and with a sudden melancholy, Nile Barrabas stood up and walked toward the shower.

It was time to go.

"HEY, GEOFF—Look, is Lee with you?"

"Nanos, what's the problem? I told you we have to be at the Surfmaster in a very short time. If you're shacking up with the usual bunch of broads, get rid of them."

"Geoff, let me talk to the doc, will you?"

Geoff Bishop held the phone out to the one female member of the SOBs and shrugged. "He insists on talking to you," he said.

They shared a moment's displeasure. Nanos was the team's least disciplined member when he was off duty. They didn't question any of the men in the field. A strike force as well trained and well disciplined as theirs had to be able to trust one another to any extreme—and the SOBs had plenty of experience to prove that there was no reason to doubt their comrades in battle or in any other tight spot. Once the R and R started, though, Nanos was off on some media image of a swinging bachelor's life.

There were the rented yachts on both coasts and most continents. There were endless women, most of them mindless, and there was plenty of drinking. The general consensus was that Nanos was worse than a grown-up adolescent when it came to the way he lived his life.

Geoff had always been different, more serious than Alex, but since Geoff had come back from a sure grave a while ago, his life with Lee had changed, and so had the two of them. If Geoff had ever been a bachelor type, it didn't show in the way he appreciated his relationship with Lee.

Geoff had been thought dead after a shoot-out with terrorists in Florida. He'd actually been taken hostage by them and held in Lebanon for months, until the SOBs had discovered his unexpected survival when they'd taken on some of the most dangerous Shiite hijackers ever.

His life since then was much less carefree than before, and so was his attachment to Lee.

The woman came across the room and took the receiver from his hand. She swept back her hair to uncover her ear. She was dressed casually in jeans and boots and a comfortable old turtleneck, the usual outfit for both of them when they were in Quebec.

"Alex, what is it?" Her voice was obviously sharp.

"Look, Doc, I just have to ask you about Billy Two."

"What's wrong with him?" Lee was suddenly more serious. She was taking the conversation more professionally now that she knew for sure that the Greek wasn't going to pull some problem out of his hat; she also had continuing concerns about the state of the full-blooded Osage who was another member of the SOBs.

"Well, I really think he's beginning to lose it more, Lee. I mean it. He's off in the Sierras doing more of these spiritual things, like meditation and all of that. You know how he talks to that god of his."

"It's more complicated than that, Alex," Lee Hatton replied in a measured voice. She certainly knew that it was.

Billy Two had been held captive in a Spetsnaz prison in Siberia during one of the SOBs' actions. The Russian secret service had subjected him to chemical torture. It had, she'd determined, driven him to the edge of an artificially induced schizophrenia.

It was during that time that Billy Two had begun to talk to what he called *Hawk Spirit*. He would still go off on a moment's notice, leaving any reality behind. Or at least he would leave behind the reality that a traditionally educated person understood.

Lee, as a scientist, found Billy Two's condition fascinating. There were parts of it that she could understand and explain clinically. The effects of the Russian chemicals were one example. She had to admit, though, that there was more to it than simply that. Something did happen inside Billy Two that was beyond Western understanding.

"Do you think he's in danger?"

"No, no, you know William Starfoot II," Nanos said, jokingly calling the Osage by his full name. "I just wonder if, you know, if he really should be going on an assignment now. I mean, he's been doing the talking a lot lately, to that hawk thing of his."

Lee was the physician of the team, and she certainly could decide whose mental state was inadequate for a mission.

She thought for a while, then decided on her course of action. "I'll talk to him with special care when we get to Hawaii, Nanos. Get him to the hotel there as soon as you can. Geoff and I can be in Honolulu right away. We'll take our own plane, and it'll mean we won't have to wait for commercial schedules. By the time you get to the Sierras and find him and then get him to LAX, we'll probably already be there. I'll give him a complete physical then.''

"Okay, Doc, you're the boss on this one. I just get worried, you know?''

The phone disconnected. Lee put the receiver down and stood still, deep in thought. She felt Geoff's hand on her shoulder. "You want to take the Lear, then?''

Geoff had come into a huge amount of money when he'd gotten out of the Lebanese captivity. Hoping against hope that Geoff was still alive, the team had always put aside his share after each one of their missions, and the accumulated savings, plus considerable interest, had left him with much more than enough to purchase the luxurious long-range jet that they kept on the private runway near the Canadian house and used to commute to the Mediterranean.

"Yes. I think so.''

She hadn't even looked at him when she'd spoken. Geoff waited for a moment, wondering if he should interrupt her thoughts, but decided against it. They'd have plenty of time on the plane. Just the two of them would be on it for many hours together.

BILLY TWO HAD GOTTEN to the peak after a three-day hike. He'd dropped the pack from his shoulder and looked around at the unrivaled splendor of the Sierra Nevada. There was nothing here to remind him of the white civilization he'd left behind. There was only the endless expanse of forest and the majestic beauty of the mountain range in his sight. All through it lived the animals that the gods had delivered to earth to give man food, clothing and companionship.

He wasn't far below the timberline, that point in the height of the earth's surface past which no trees could grow. Here there were still many trees with huge trunks soaring toward the heavens. There was also the stream.

He went over and squatted next to the small flow of water that seemed to come out of nothingness. It was escaping from a fissure in a large piece of granite. Surely it must spring from a natural artesian well, he assumed. He cupped his hands and lifted a draft of the liquid to his lips.

It tasted incredibly good. There was a clarity to it that water from a tap in the city could never even approximate. Billy Two retrieved more of the water and sipped it, then took handfuls and poured them over his head, letting it clean his body of the sweat that had poured out of him during the trek up the mountainside.

He was as close as he was going to get, he decided. His map had promised this spring, and he had known that the natural state of the land would have been maintained here, far from the tourist developments that were slowly marching from the edges of the forests into the primeval glory of the continent.

He stood up and began to slowly strip off his clothing. Billy Two was there to commune with his gods again. They wouldn't want a man to appear before them clad in the remnants of a foreign civilization.

When he was naked, he reaffirmed his pledge to himself and then went to work.

He spent the next three days cutting down brush and dead tree limbs for the fire. These dried pieces of wood would burn hotter and faster than any others. He also found straight stands of younger trees for lumber.

He didn't eat a single thing for the whole three days. He subsisted on the water from the stream. It wasn't easy. His stomach rebelled often, growling its anger and clutching him painfully with cramps as it was emptied of all the processed foods—and poisons—it had come to depend upon.

Billy Two would come to his gods in purity, just as he had to approach them naked, without ostentatious clothing.

At night, he slept in a sleeping bag made of animal pelts, the product of his own hunting and curing. The bag was much more comfortable than the ones made of strange artificial fibers in the white man's factory.

After the third night, he had grown to love the bag even more. Sleep had come more easily as his stomach slowly accepted its emptiness. The odors of his body and the skins had merged together. His lungs had been able to use the clean air of the high peaks to purge themselves of many of the pollutants contaminating them.

The anticipation of the next night had also helped him sleep. Billy Two knew he was getting closer to the time when it would all happen.

He spent the day constructing the steam hut. He'd learned to do the primitive carpentry when he'd been a young boy, before his father, an oil millionaire who'd retreated to a decadent life-style in Oklahoma, had tried to turn him into a white by sending him to "good" schools and introducing him to the sons of other "good" families.

The slender trunks of the young trees were held together with a twine that Billy Two had made from the long strands of vines in the forests. Leaves and mud had been mulched together to create a kind of thick plaster covering the trunks. There was only the smallest hole at the top of the hut for some circulation.

Other Native Americans might have used hallucinogens to induce the proper frame of mind. The peoples of the Southwest were fond of the magic mushrooms that grew in their deserts and of the peyote buttons that flowered on the tops of some of their cacti. Those had negative connotations to Billy Two. He'd seen the danger of drugs too often. He wanted none of it.

Besides, his fasting was going to have nearly the same effect. He felt his stomach, harder even than it had been before he'd begun—and his muscular body had been very hard then. There was nothing in it, only the constant flow of fluids removing the last vestiges of poison in his urine as he continued to flush himself with water.

His head was already purified. He knew that. He could tell by the spells of lightness that he went through. A man in good shape, he wasn't used to having waves of faintness attack him after a spell of hard labor, but Billy Two had come to expect those.

It would soon be over, though, and he wasn't concerned.

He was worried about this adventure of his. What if the Russians had really destroyed his mind? What if there was no Hawk Spirit? Was he doomed to live as a crazy man? That was his purpose there on the mountaintop. He was there to find out if his gods were real or delusions. He wanted proof. He *needed* proof. If he used the ancient ways of the Osage to call on the spirits, and they responded, then he might have an answer to his questions.

He'd built the hut over a smooth expanse of hard rock. On it he piled stacks of the dry wood he'd gathered. He had skins full of water from the stream. He was ready.

He pulled the deerskin flap of the hut closed behind him. He sat down on the rock. He had a flint and used it to spark the fuel to fire. He let it burn for two hours, constantly feeding it more wood.

The temperature inside the closed hut rose higher and higher. Sweat poured off Billy Two, coursing down his skin, dripping off his elbows and his thighs. The rock was heating more and more. There could be nothing left in him but purity now.

When the rocks were red-hot, Billy Two began to sprinkle water over them, creating clouds of steam that came inside his lungs and washed them even more.

He felt his mind slipping, going away from the momentary trap of his body and soaring up to seek the gods. He was doing what his grandfathers had taught him to do, and experiencing what they had told him would happen if he followed the righteous way of the Osage.

His mind was moving, up and away from his physical being, it was reaching, reaching....

"I've come for you," Billy Two heard his voice saying. It was weird; he hadn't told it to talk. He waited to see if there would be an answer.

"You have come to the wrong place, my son."

It was there! Hawk Spirit had come to him.

"I've climbed the highest mountain to get closer to your world," Billy Two said. "I have removed everything from my body that belongs to the white man, and I come to you as a pure Osage."

"You have come to the wrong place, my son."

Billy Two was confused. He studied the clouds of steam that surrounded him and could see in the faintest of outlines the form of Hawk Spirit in front of him. He would never be able to tell a white man what the god looked like. It had a form that could be understood only by the people it guarded—the Osage.

"I want to join you," Billy Two said suddenly, ignoring the repeated statement from the god. "I want to come to the place where the gods live." If there really was a Hawk Spirit, Billy Two had to be with him!

"You have no right to join the gods."

"Please!" Billy Two felt a new liquid on his skin; tears were pouring down his cheeks. "Please let me join the circle of the Osage in the heavens!"

"What will you do for the gods that they would have you join them?"

"Anything! Everything!"

"My son, speak slowly, carefully. The promises of the gods are forever, and the prayers you make are

sometimes answered. It is not time for you to come to us. You have our work to do on the earth now. You must prove yourself."

"I want to join you," Billy Two cried out once more. He was feeling the loneliness of the warrior left alone. He, like the great men of all times, was trying to merge himself and his fate with his gods. He couldn't stand the limitations of his human form. "Take me to you and let me serve you. I'll be a servant at your side. Let me enter heaven, and I'll be your slave for eternity."

"A warrior is not a slave to anyone!" The voice of Hawk Spirit was so angry and so adamant that Billy Two recoiled from it. *"A warrior performs as a warrior must. You had your duty to do to your gods. Your duty is on earth. If you perform adequately, you will be rewarded appropriately."*

"You will let me into heaven and you will let me sit beside you!" Billy Two cried again, because he heard Hawk Spirit offer him salvation.

"You will spend your time on earth. You must save my temple."

"Your temple? But where? You have no temple but the heart of the Osage." Billy Two was confused. He didn't understand the message his meditation was giving him.

"I have many lives and many forms and many peoples. The Osage are my chosen here, on this huge island, but I have no limits. The wings of Hawk Spirit span the world and beyond it. My temple is defiled. You will save it."

"Alone? By myself?"

"Your brothers will guide you."

"Brothers? I have no brothers. Ever since I first met you, I have been alone. I have my comrades, but none who understand Hawk Spirit, none who believe in it."

"You do have brothers. You have teachers yet to fill your mind and your spirit. A large bird will take you to them. When you are with them, you will find my temple, and you will save it. You will find true believers, and you will use your skills to protect them."

Billy Two was astonished by the message. He sat there and studied the billowing clouds, waiting for the next words from Hawk Spirit. He heard some noise, something foreign and intrusive, and thought for a while that it was the sound of the beating of Hawk Spirit's wings.

The sound repeated over and over again, and it got constantly louder. Whop...Whop...Whop...

Then the noise was exploding inside Billy Two's head, pounding away inside his skull.

"Hey, Billy Two, you in there?"

Billy Two's mind couldn't take in the strangeness of what it was hearing. There was something familiar about it, but what could it be? What did it have to do with Hawk Spirit?

The flap to his hut was pulled open, and bright sunlight came into the darkness, hurting his eyes and making him cover them with his hands for protection. There were hard, callused hands on his shoulders and under his arms, pulling and dragging him away from the heat and the smoke and the fire, taking him away from Hawk Spirit.

Then there was sudden coolness as the mountain air enveloped his naked body. Someone was holding water to his lips. "Just a little, don't guzzle it, just a little . . ."

Billy Two felt a trickle of the springwater flow down his throat and into his belly. Then he was being wrapped in something strange, certainly not his skins. When he finally got his eyes open again and adjusted to the light, he could see his friend, Alex Nanos. The Greek was pulling a pair of pants on Billy Two, cotton uniform slacks that had nothing to do with an Osage warrior's communion with his god.

There was someone else, whom Billy Two didn't know, helping with a shirt, and then they were both getting boots on his feet. "Is he okay? Want me to radio ahead to the hospital?" the Strange One was asking Alex.

"Billy Two, you okay?" Nanos was asking.

Billy Two was smiling, grinning with enthusiasm. "We're going to save the temple," he said. "I'm just fine, Alex, just fine."

"I don't know, mister, I think we better radio the hospital. I think this guy's lost it."

Billy Two ignored the comment. He was looking at the helicopter the pair of them had used to come up to the mountain to get him. It was a bird, a great bird, just as Hawk Spirit had said it would be. His god lived! It wasn't any figment of his imagination, and it wasn't a mental illness. His Hawk Spirit was real!

Billy Two pushed the other two men away from himself. "I don't need this bull," he said. He stood up, wobbly at first, but quickly got his balance. He finished dressing himself and began to move around, first putting out the fire with large doses of water to make sure there was no flame left to spread and damage the forest. Then he retrieved his pack and his sleeping bag. "I'm ready, Alex. I guess we got work to do, huh? That's the reason you came and got me, isn't it?"

"Yeah, Billy Two, that's it." The Greek studied the transformed Osage and wondered, yet once again, if his friend was going to be okay. "We got to go to Hawaii first, to meet up with Nile and the rest of them."

"Then?"

"I don't know, Billy Two. You know how it is. We get called and we answer. It's the soldier in us."

"We got a real good assignment this time, Alex—I just know it!"

The pilot and Alex exchanged looks as they watched the Osage climb into the helicopter and sit quietly waiting for them. Nanos finally shrugged. "Let's get out of here. We got a flight to catch at LAX."

4

The team didn't physically stand up and salute when Nile Barrabas walked into the room, but they did come to attention mentally.

The penthouse suite of the Surfmaster Hotel on Waikiki Beach was one of the most expensive pieces of real estate in the world, but the minds of the men and woman who made up the SOBs weren't on the luxury of their setting. It was time for their briefing. They were going to hear the details of the mission they were about to undertake and to receive the information that they'd have to have in order to fulfill that mission.

Nile nodded to them curtly. Lee Hatton studied him from the back of the room where she sat with Geoff, and wondered—as she did from time to time—about the tensions and stress that leadership brought to a man like Barrabas. From that moment on, he would be in charge of their lives. They would follow every one of his orders without question. It was all in their training, and it was what made them the best mercenaries in the world.

There was, in a strange way, a relief from responsibility in their position. They weren't being paid to decide which one of them took what risks. They weren't going to make decisions that would determine who—

if any—of the enemy would die. The weight of those decisions was all on Nile's shoulders.

Most men would have cracked from it all long ago. But Nile had seemed to be on top of it all, always. In most ways, Lee thought, it was proof of the worth and strength of the man that he was able to consistently uphold the team and keep it on track. There was a bit of humanity missing in him, though. She watched for glimpses of it and saw none as he opened up his briefing book, which was actually a leather-covered folder with carefully maintained pages of notes in it.

She knew that something of Nile was being withheld; she just didn't know what. Geoff shifted in his seat on the other side of the couch, and their eyes met briefly. She brought her mind back from its rambling. It was time to pay attention to the team leader.

"This is one of the least interesting assignments we've ever had," Barrabas said. There was a touch of displeasure, perhaps even distaste, in his voice as he spoke. "Jessup's people in Washington have a problem with a renegade European science team that's at work in Matali, in the Pacific.

"It's an isolated country; the closest neighbor is Tahiti. The place is a favorite with American cruise ships, and that's about all. It's one of those tropical paradises that can effortlessly supply food for its people but not the goodies a lot of its leaders want—the Rolex-and-Rolls-Royce syndrome we've seen in so many small-time dictators appears to be in full force in Matali.

"The head of the government—a military man named General Falanu—is the greedy one. He's West

Point—'' That brought even more distaste into Barrabas's voice; he obviously wasn't pleased that the man was a graduate of his own alma mater. ''But very soft. He removed a weak civilian government a few years ago and would be well on the road to total dictatorship if it weren't for a powerful priest caste that evidently claims almost absolute loyalty from the vast majority of the people.

''Matali has rented one of its small out islands to the European company we're supposed to...interfere with.''

''Nile, are you telling us that we're going to be common industrial criminals?'' Claude Hayes was obviously unhappy with what he was hearing. The huge black man was a physical equal to Barrabas, over six feet tall and with the same bulky, well-maintained muscles.

Nile took a deep breath. ''Our job is to do our job,'' he said impatiently. ''It appears that this operation is a real threat to elements in the American space program. I'm not going to second-guess NASA or the Pentagon on their priorities.

''Obviously, nothing from official Washington can be implicated in any operation like this one....''

'''Bout time someone got that message,'' Hayes said with renewed disgust.

Nile ignored him that round and continued, ''The main thing is to make the space base inoperative for a significant time and to do it in such a way that the United States doesn't appear to be involved.''

''What other elements figure in the island's situation?'' Liam O'Toole asked. The Irishman, who had grown up in the middle of the sectarian battles of Ireland, was the team member most conscious of the possible complexities in any country's internal affairs.

"There's some conflict with various fishing nations about the country's claim of a two-hundred-mile limit. The big fishing fleets—from Japan, Peru, the U.S. and elsewhere—challenge the legality. Seems there are many dozens of specks of soil and rock over which Matali claims sovereignty, and it measures its control of fishing rights from the shore of each one. That would give it a claim over a huge expanse of the Pacific, almost as large a water surface area as New Zealand's, in fact, and the rest of the countries don't like it.

"They're slinging it out in the World Court in The Hague, and in lots of hit-and-run small-time battles between one another on the sea as well. It's potentially a part of all this, but we don't know how."

"Nile, have you figured out how we're going to handle this one?"

"No. Quite frankly, Claude, I don't have a complete scenario drawn out for once. The intelligence reports we have are very incomplete, much more sketchy than we're used to getting from Jessup and his contacts.

"Matali just wasn't considered important enough to warrant much attention up till now, and no one kept track of its situation very well. Even our satellite maps—usually perfect—are inadequate for some reason.

"We have plenty of time on this one. Nothing dramatic is going to happen in the next week. I've discovered that there are some resort islands far from the main island that can be rented. One of them's owned by an extremely wealthy man, somebody known to the senator. It even has its own landing strip, sufficient for your Lear jet, Geoff."

Barrabas paused, then said, "I want the main group of us to go there. Geoff, you and Lee are going to drop us off, then proceed to the main island. You have perfect cover as tourists, rich young Americans on vacation."

Nile paced about for a few steps, eyeing the rest of his team, then turned back to Lee Hatton and the Canadian pilot. "You can take the material I have and you can use it as a base to check its accuracy and make any other observations you come across.

"Nanos, you take Billy Two and fly to Matali via commercial jet. I have reservations all lined up for a Qantas flight this afternoon. There are papers here showing you're a seaman out of San Diego. I don't understand the whole thing that's going on with these fishing rights.

"I know that the issues of who can commercially fish where is something that can involve many million dollars in profits, but I just don't see who's got what to gain here in Matali. Knowing as much as you do about boats and fishing, you can be our eyes and ears on that part of the operation."

"But, ah, Nile, you sure you want me to take Billy Two?"

Nanos seemed uncomfortable with the idea. Barrabas blinked in surprise. The Greek and the Indian had been a pair since the SOBs had been established. He didn't want Nanos to go into an unknown area alone, without any backup, and he'd simply assumed that Alex would want Billy Two to accompany him.

"Yes, Alex, that's what I said."

"Yeah, sure," Nanos replied, obviously not about to argue with the boss on that one.

As they went through a rundown of schedule and location and studied the incomplete maps that Nile had of the Matali archipelago, Barrabas was vaguely aware of something going on between Nanos and Billy Two.

It wasn't real conflict; if it had been that, Nile would have known different ways to handle it. Instead, it simply seemed that Billy Two was even spacier than usual.

Nile looked over at Lee Hatton and saw that she, too, was studying the two men and doing just as much to hide her interest as he was. He relaxed then. He was confident that Lee would have told him if there was something crucially wrong. Since she had made no move to speak to him about the two men, she hadn't seen anything that her doctor's training indicated should be interfered with. He made a mental note to speak to her when they were alone on the resort island. They'd figure out a way to examine the situation when they had a chance. For now, the basic plan was operative.

"BILLY TWO, for God's sake, man, just have a drink with me, will you?"

Billy Two looked blankly at Alex Nanos and smiled vacantly. He shook his head no.

"Billy Two, what's with you? You're acting like some kind of zombie. There are skirts here that should be making your blood pressure go crazy. You go on assignment to work undercover in one of the tropical paradises in the world, and you don't want to go to bars and down booze. You just walk around this place like some kind of nut, smiling at strangers."

"They may be my brothers," Billy Two said quietly. "I must prepare my mind and my body for Hawk Spirit's followers."

"Billy Two, listen to me! If Barrabas finds out you're losing the few nuts you have in your skull, I don't know what the hell's going to happen to you. Stop with the religious talk, will you? It's not as though we're going on a pilgrimage, Billy Two."

"I'm here because Hawk Spirit wants me here," Billy Two said slowly, in a tone of voice that didn't even seem to be responding to what Nanos was saying. "I'm going to go back outside now, Alex. Okay? You'll be all right here in the bar?"

"Yeah, yeah, Billy Two, go on, do your thing." Alex shook his head, as though in defeat. "Just get back to the hotel room later tonight, will you? Please? I'll handle the spy stuff here in the town."

Billy Two stood up and walked out of the bar where they'd been sitting and talking. The place had smelled of white men—their chemically treated tobacco and their alcohol. Billy Two had been uncomfortable with it all, just as he had felt claustrophobic on the jumbo jetliner that had deposited them and a couple of hundred other people at the island's airport last night.

He kept imagining himself back on his mountaintop, talking to Hawk Spirit, naked to the elements and in touch with himself, his gods, his heritage. Everything else seemed such a pale imitation of life since those glorious moments.

He walked around Matali. The people were certainly pleasant-looking, and they even seemed familiar to him in some strange way. Their skin was the same tawny color as his own, and he saw in their eyes the same slight slant, not truly Mongoloid, but not the ovalness of the Caucasian, either.

They wore very little clothing, something for which he envied them. The women seemed content with a saronglike garment that barely went to their knees, and a loose halter top. The men most often made do with walking shorts; most of them didn't even bother with a T-shirt. There was no need to protect oneself from the elements in that climate.

They were all obvious in their interest in him. Billy Two had let his black hair grow in the past few months until it now fell over his shoulders in the traditional long style of the Osage. He had hated the idea of getting back into Western clothes when Nanos had brought him down from the mountaintop, but he'd compromised.

He wore heavy boots with steel toes, which he actually considered a form of weapon and thus necessary while he was on assignment. He also had on khaki slacks that approximated his uniform pants from the military. But he wasn't wearing a shirt. Instead, he'd fashioned a deerskin vest for himself. He wore it over his bare chest.

Billy Two had long ago pierced his right ear while on a drunk in a European seaport, thinking it would be a kick to look like a pirate. Recently the Osage had opened his earlobe, and now he had a small feather hanging from it, one he'd gotten from a zoo in California, just outside the cages where they'd trapped the peregrine hawks that used to rule the skies of the United States. The small feather was a totem to him, a reminder of his dedication to Hawk Spirit.

It was just one more element that made him stand out on the streets of Matali. He was easily a foot taller than most of the people there, and the hair and the nearly naked chest would have been noticeable enough, but the feather earring really did it.

Small boys were following him at a respectful distance. He was aware of them and wasn't bothered by their presence. They could even have made fun of him if they'd wanted to: Billy Two wasn't going to resist the taunts of children.

He was actually wondering why Hawk Spirit had brought him to that place. He never doubted that it had. There were no mistakes in the way Hawk Spirit moved. He was sure of that since his faith had been proven. There could only be mankind's inability to see his wisdom that made Hawk Spirit's decisions invisible.

Matali was built around a splendid natural harbor. The houses, for the most part, sat on a plain that wrapped around the arc of the port. Behind them there were sharp inclines as the hills of the island climbed up toward the volcanic peaks dominating the interior.

Billy Two, with his young entourage, moved to the edge of the village. There was a tropical forest there, or rather a forest that would have turned densely tropical if it hadn't been so carefully cared for.

The fruit trees, which were the most common form of vegetation here, were obviously well tended. The brush that would have grown up around their trunks was cut down, and the trees were spaced so perfectly that they had obviously been thinned out. There was a whole marketful of different species. Besides breadfruit and mangoes, which were native to that part of the world, there were also orange and lime and other citrus trees that must have been imported.

The trees appeared to be part of the common property of the island. There was no sign of private ownership, and occasionally Billy Two would see a man or a woman nonchalantly moving through the groves and picking whatever he or she desired from the branches with obvious freedom, never looking around to check if anyone else was watching.

The farther he moved from the village, the thicker the foliage got, but it never returned to a truly primitive state. The care the plants were given was still evident.

Billy Two had been walking on an unpaved road. There hadn't been any sign of civilized housing since he'd left the village's structures. Suddenly he came upon a large clearing.

The boys who were still behind him broke into a loud and cheerful chatter when they saw the structure. One of them felt bold enough to come right up to Billy Two and pull on the fringe of his vest. "Our temple," the kid said proudly.

Billy Two didn't answer him. He couldn't say a word. Because there, right before him, in front of the building that was obviously the cathedral of the local religion, was an enormous stone sculpture of Hawk Spirit, just the way he appeared in Billy Two's visions.

"Is there a priest here, kid?" Billy Two forced himself to ask. Speaking right then was one of the most difficult things he'd ever had to do. He was trapped in something between awe and reverence, fear and exultation at having come across anything as grand as that statue.

"I'll get him for you. The old one cares for the temple. He'll be here."

As the boy ran away, Billy Two screwed up all his courage and moved a few steps closer to the statue. He remembered the photographs he'd seen of the enormous primitive stone sculptures on Easter Island. Scientists and archaeologists had spent lifetimes trying to figure out their meaning and their origin, because it seemed impossible that mere human beings could have carted the huge boulders necessary to create them up to the tops of the hills where they stood. Easter Islanders were considered too primitive to have understood the tools that would have been necessary to do the work otherwise.

This portrait of Hawk Spirit had some of the same primeval look about it, but that didn't deny the obvious grace and beauty and the work that had gone into it. The thing was monumental, not just in its size, but also in its grandeur.

Billy Two dared take a couple more steps and put a hand on the surface of the stone. He felt something move through his entire body and tried to remember when he'd had that feeling before.

On the mountaintop! When Hawk Spirit had come to speak to him! That was when he'd felt that way.

Billy Two didn't even make a decision; he dropped to his knees in front of his idol and stared at the face.

"My son, you know the great god?"

The voice behind him broke into his prayers and made him suddenly self-conscious. Billy Two stood up quickly and turned to face a very small and very old man who was wearing a kind of skirt and who had beads hanging around his neck.

Before Billy Two could answer, the priest's mouth opened in amazement. He was studying the side of Billy Two's face. A wizened hand reached up and was barely able to touch the hawk feather that hung from the Osage's ear.

"Yes, yes," the man whispered, "you know the god, of course you do." The man pulled back his hand and then used it to take hold of Billy Two's forearm. "Come with me—you and I have much to talk about. I've waited so many years for you to appear. It is so good that you did come before I died."

"THE GOD YOU CALL Hawk Spirit left Matali when the whites came," the priest was explaining. "He was disgusted with us all for our inability to protect his temples and his holy places."

They were drinking herbal tea in the priest's simple lodgings.

"He wouldn't tolerate our unwillingness to fight, and without him we became unable to fight. That is the great gap in our souls, my son, that Hawk Spirit has left. But you have come to bring him back to us. It was written that one of our warriors would do so."

"But I'm not one of your warriors. I'm an Osage, from the United States. I'm not from Matali."

The priest nodded. "It's said that many of our people left this island in the time before my great-great-great-father's memory. They left on war canoes to explore the outer reaches of the world. They took with them a totem of Hawk Spirit so they could conquer any people they found. But they never came back.

"It was said that the gods told our people not to worry. That group of warriors had survived and had conquered and were much feared in their new land. They would rejoin us someday when we would need them.

"They must be your ancestors, the warriors from Matali who went to the east so long ago."

Billy Two tried to grab hold of as much traditional knowledge as he could. He knew perfectly well that historians thought it was likely that many of the ancestors of the Native Americans had come from the Orient, either across a land bridge that had once joined Siberia with Alaska or else in large boats that had sailed across the Pacific.

Was this really the land of his ancestors? He thought back to the similarities he'd sensed between himself and the people here. They'd been so subtle, but they'd been real. And, above all, there was the god, the one the priest was telling him was the same as Hawk Spirit.

"You said Hawk Spirit's temple was defiled?"

"There were more than one. On this island there were many, in fact, tributes to the warlike tribesmen who once ruled the island and all the others within reach.

"But the main temple was on an island not too far from here. For many years it was not touched by the Westerners who'd done so much damage to the rest of Matali. It was on an island where there were no people living. We who were devoted to the god would go there when we could, without letting the Westerners know so they would follow us.

"When your adopted country—" the priest said weightily, evidently unwilling to admit that Billy Two wasn't one of the Matali natives himself "—entered the great war against the Japanese, they took over the island. They didn't know what they were doing when they built their hospital on the site of the god's temple. We took it as a sign that they were the chosen ones because they picked that spot.

"We cared for those men, but we never told them about the secrets of the temple. The underground passages where relics of our religion are kept were never discovered by them. We wanted to resurrect our religion when they left. We weren't able to.

"'The son of a pig who calls himself the president of Matali sold it to new Westerners, and they've torn the temple down.'' The old priest looked up at the huge statue and seemed to ask its forgiveness. "It was the real temple. With it went our hope of Hawk Spirit coming back to Matali, ever. But I was so foolish to doubt his promise that the warrior would come and doubt the legend that said that the band of fighting men who went to the East would come back when they were needed.

"It is you, young man, who will save us."

Billy Two's mind echoed with the words Hawk Spirit had spoken to him on the mountaintop in California. "Tell me more about the temple that has been desecrated and what we must do to save it."

5

Nile Barrabas was still unpacking his gear when the radio came to life. Nate Beck had barely finished putting the communications center together when it happened, but he had his headgear on at once and was talking into the microspeaker attached to his head, much like a telephone operator's.

"Hello, who is it?" The radio had an internal scrambling device that made it unnecessary for any of them on the same frequency to use code or talk in technical terminology. The members of the SOBs were the only ones who could understand whatever went out over the airwaves between them.

"Geoff here. Let me talk to the boss."

Barrabas walked over and took the controls from Beck. "What's up, Bishop?" he asked in his straightforward manner.

"Evidently a lot, Nile. We tried to take a spin over Devil's Land, just as you asked, but our equipment picked up a definite warning. We were locked in by someone's radar. It read as though it could have been a tracking device for a missile operation, and we weren't about to test that theory, as unarmed as we were."

Barrabas didn't argue with his man's good sense. "Fine, Geoff. Continue as planned with your undercover work on Matali, and we'll check into this on our own."

Barrabas didn't look at Nate as he handed the communications man back the gear. His forehead was wrinkled with concern.

"Nile, I had a chance to look at those satellite charts you gave me to study while we were en route over here," Beck said. "I thought for a long while that they were just what the meteorological teams had told you: probably volcanic activity had produced a dust cover from residual discharge into the atmosphere and that was the reason none of the satellite pictures were clear enough for us to get a good reading.

"But this missile thing . . . it has me thinking."

"Go on," Barrabas prompted, always interested in anything Beck had to say. The man's ability to understand machines and decipher their products was uncanny. There were times when the other team members swore that Nate didn't have a brain, just a megabyte hard disk in his skull.

"Well—" Beck said, more tentative than usual "—satellite photographs are usually good enough to see through most things. If there had been a real suspicion that there was something of great international importance going on on that island, there could even have been some infrared pictures taken. Our technology is so refined that we have that down.

"I'm going to assume that it hasn't been done because no one at NASA or in the Pentagon understood that the island's activities were that interesting. It's late in the game to ask them to go around and do that for us now.

"Again, they simply didn't have any reason to question their assumptions before about the cloud cover. But I do, if that island has defenses sophisticated enough to have lock-on missile radar.

"There have been some top-secret studies done on using solar energy to create diffusion in the atmosphere that would interfere with a photographic process in a way that would be hard to discern."

"Beck, talk English."

"They're playing with mirrors, Nile. To be as simplistic as possible, they're using some very high-tech tricks to reflect the sun back onto the lens of the satellite cameras in such a way that no photographic image can be taken. I think it would work just as well— maybe even better—if they *did* use infrared cameras. Those are dependent on heat sources for their images.

"Whoever is out there playing games with this little island is doing it with some very big toys, the kind that only the really big boys have."

Nile swore silently. So this was Jessup's idea of a "simple" mission, one with a minimum of danger? Barrabas wasn't surprised. Trusting the Fixer wasn't something that the team had specialized in for a long time. He was their agent, nothing else. He got the assignments, took his cut, and that was all. They were the ones left to do the dirty work. If anything, Jessup's assurances that the job would be a piece of cake had made Barrabas all the more alert.

The men and Lee hadn't been allowed any relaxation of discipline just because they were approaching a reportedly civilian target not attached to a major power. As soon as they'd finished their briefing in Hawaii and begun their trip down to Matali, they had entered the special mind-set of the soldier in a war zone. They'd all gone through enough before to have learned that the most innocent-looking location could still mean big trouble for them.

"I think we're going to have to go in there for some reconnaissance," Nile announced. "The one thing we have to be able to count on is decent intelligence." It was the one thing that every commander knew; Barrabas thought to himself: you could have the best fighting force in the world, but without the knowledge of what you were entering and who you were going to meet there, you would only end up needlessly sacrificing your men.

"Good thing we brought that speedboat," Nate said.

Nile nodded. "It was obviously going to be necessary in any operation that had so much island-hopping to it," he answered. "Let's go see if Liam and Claude have it operational yet."

The two men left the house and walked toward the pier that stuck out into the lagoon of the small island. The island they'd rented was the private retreat of one of the great names in Hollywood. It was rumored that the star would come down to his small place, thousands of miles from the nearest gossip columnist or *Entertainment Tonight* video camera, accompanied by a dozen aspiring starlets. If they would spend the month or two he requested of them living out his fantasies, they would get a boost in their careers when they got back to California.

His fantasies weren't simple little sexual plays, either. He wanted to live the life of a South Seas potentate. The women were dressed in grass skirts, the like of which no female wore on the islands anymore, and went bare-breasted over the grounds.

Traversing the well-kept lawns, Nile and Beck proceeded to the waterside. The utter privacy of the place was its main attraction for them. It had wind-generated power for their needs, which weren't complex, except for their communication gear. The same windmills served to power pumps delivering fresh water to the surface of the island and filling the Olympic size swimming pool located behind the house.

At the pier, Liam O'Toole and Claude Hayes were working on the final touches to the sleek speedboat that had been brought over by air in pieces. The private airstrip was a handy addition to the island's other resources.

"It's ready, Nile," Liam announced, running his bare arm over his forehead to wipe off the sweat. He obviously didn't want to use his greased-up hands to do the job.

Liam was a native of Ireland and had the pale skin of a Gaelic son. His hair was already showing more red highlights than usual after exposure to the equatorial rays. Claude was a dark-skinned man of African descent. His skin shone with sweat as he worked in the tropical heat.

Their completed project was in the water beside the small pier. It was a Formula One, the same racing boat that was so popular with the Coast Guard, drug smugglers and any other armed force interested in extreme speed and not worried about the nice things in cruiseware.

But the SOBs' boat was different in one significant way. Like all the others, it had the smooth-skinned hull that ensured it would move through the water with the least possible friction drag, and it was powered by twin engines, two big Volvo motors that gave it a top speed of more than eighty-five knots per hour. The uniqueness of the craft wasn't even apparent to the eye, and it wouldn't be noted by a trained sailor, either. It was in the material used to construct the hull, and the casings for the engines. It was all made of Kevlar, the same high-tech synthetic used in bullet-proof vests.

Someone had discovered another unique application for Kevlar: it couldn't be detected by radar.

The Second World War has shown the fighting forces of the world the importance of radar. The primitive forms of the new science that the British and Germans had used against each other had been one of the main factors in the outcome of that war. It had been the radar of the U-boats that had made them such a fearsome power in the North Atlantic, allowing them to find and destroy convoy after convoy of Allied shipping. And British radar had allowed the English precious warning when the Nazi bombers were coming across the channel to attack cities during the Battle of Britain.

Once the cold war had begun, the superpowers had sent their scientists to work to figure out what other advantages radar could give them. When the new discoveries in that field were coupled with the fast-moving finds in the computer field, a kind of mega-scale video game started to take over the minds of military strategists. The distinction between unmanned missiles and warplanes with human pilots at the controls began to blur.

But as soon as radar was advanced enough to guide flight and the aiming of weapons, technology had turned on itself and begun to devise means to undermine its original invention. The best-known, worst-kept secret in American aviation history was the Stealth bomber, a plane built of supersecret materials that defied radar's ability to find it. Kevlar, as it turned out, had many of the same qualities.

"It's all set if we ever need it, Nile," Liam said. He flashed the SOB leader a big smile, the white of his teeth all the brighter in contrast to the grime on his face.

"Tonight." Barrabas looked over the Formula One. He could see how it got the name "cigar boat" from the narrow aerodynamic styling. The engines took up most of the space on board the craft, but there would still be room for the four of them and light weapons, as well.

"No need for anything fancy. This is just reconnaissance," Barrabas said. "We should be able to go right up close to the shore. According to the map, there's a beach on one side of the island, away from the harbor that's usually the point where people come ashore. We'll use that beach and see what's there.

"You men better get some rest. We're going to need it if we're going to be in top shape for this."

"Reconnaissance, huh?" Claude said, idly scratching his side where the salt water he'd been standing in had dried and left a slightly itchy crust. "Seems like we could have more fun than that, Nile."

"Not this time around," Barrabas insisted. "I want much more information about this operation than we have before I commit us to any action."

"It's that bad, Nile?" Liam asked. "You're that unsure of what the Fixer and his friends have gotten us into this time?"

"I didn't say that," Nile answered stiffly, but not in a way to imply any defensiveness. He was simply acting the leader in the operation the best way he knew how. He gave orders and expected them to be followed with the respect he'd earned from these men over the years. "I just want to know what's up.

"Now come on, if this thing is in shape, leave it and let's go into the house and get some sleep. It's about fifteen nautical miles to the other island. This thing should make it in no time. I want full cover of darkness, though, and we're lucky that there's no moon out tonight. We get some chow at midnight. Get ourselves ready immediately after that, and we should be able to pull out of here by one hundred hours."

"You got it, Nile," Claude answered for all three of them. They didn't ever argue with him about any of the details, even if they seemed minor. Making decisions was the prerogative of the commander in the field, and they knew it.

THE VOLVO ENGINES on the cigar boat whispered as their combined horsepower propelled the Kevlar-constructed craft over the swells of the Pacific Ocean.

The four of them were all in night cammy. They wore black cotton shorts and black long-sleeved T-shirts. Their faces, bare legs and hands were coated with dark grease to make sure that there was no perspiration to reflect the least light.

On their feet they wore light boots. In their hands they carried Mini M-16s, rapid-fire and easy-to-carry automatic rifles with which they were all intimately familiar. The weapon could stand the ocean voyage they were making; it could even tolerate being held underwater when they landed, if necessary, so long as they remembered to dump any trapped water out of the barrel. If they didn't, the thing could blow up like a sight gag in a Laurel and Hardy movie, making them the biggest kind of jokers—dead ones.

Devil's Land came into vague sight in the moonless night. They could make out the tall peaks of the volcanic island against the darkness. It was actually too easy to do so; there seemed to be some source of light inside the mountain that gave an eerie outline to the peaks. The map had indicated that the easiest place for them to approach would be from the north side, the edge of the island opposite its harbor. Here, by a waterfall, would be a tiny beach.

The Volvos purred even more softly as Nate pulled in the throttle and began to make the easy entry into the inlet. The other three men were up, their legs spread apart for balance and their eyes scanning the horizon for any sight of a welcoming party.

There was none. Nate guided the Kevlar boat right up to the land where they stepped over the craft's bow and jumped directly onto the hard black sand of the beach.

Nile, Claude and Liam pulled their rifles over their shoulders, and then each took hold of the cigar boat and heaved it up on the shore until they were sure it would be secure. The tide was going out, and there was no danger of the boat drifting off.

Nate was going to stay with it, in any event. He still had his Mini M-16 cradled in his hands as he swept the area around the landing; that would be his assignment during the reconnaissance mission. He stopped only momentarily to give the other three a traditional thumbs-up sign, wishing them good luck.

Nile led Claude and Liam toward the waterfall. The noise of the rushing water made it unnecessary for them to practice the usual stealth they'd trained for. Nature was providing the background music for the occasion, and it was giving them all the freedom they'd ever need.

The waterfall had created a series of platforms in the volcanic rock. The three men, all expertly trained in mountain climbing, easily ascended the slope of the island.

They were barely prepared when they reached the plateau at the top, having approached it so suddenly.

There was a pool of water, surprisingly placid given the rushing of the falls that originated there. Across it was the space station. Everything was extremely brightly lit. The area in front of them, in fact, seemed almost in daylight, even though they knew it was well after midnight.

"Holy shit," was all Claude could say.

"We should have brought Nate," Barrabas responded. "He could have picked up a lot of information on the rockets."

"Nothing really, Nile," Claude answered. "It's essentially the same thing as our own."

"We can pick up what we really need," Liam said, scanning the activity that was going on around the base.

There were easily two hundred men, at least half of them armed with what looked like Karlsrupa automatic rifles. The Swedish weapons were one of the favorite firearms in the world—for those who could get them. The neutral Swedes were awfully fussy about just who bought their armaments. An export license for the Karlsrupas was worth a fortune to someone who was willing to circumvent the law and deliver them, no questions asked.

There were some buildings off to the south of the clearing that seemed oddly old in the context of the ostentatious modernism of the rest of the base. "Those must have been built during the Second World War," Nile noted. They were clearly being used for the living quarters of the men who were working on the base.

Off to one side was a very modern building, one whose roof sprouted all kinds of radar tracking equipment. Some of the screens were revolving rapidly, picking up signals from the skies. Opposite that building was a series of rocket batteries.

"That's what Geoff picked up when he got too close," Liam said, indicating the missiles. Nile nodded agreement. He recognized the weapons, which were French-made, as one of the most advanced air defense systems in the world.

Claude finally said the obvious. "This is pretty heavy, Nile. I mean, this is no little picnic. These boys are after some big game, and I'm not even sure I want to know what it is."

"But we're going to find out," Nile answered unemotionally. "We've begun this, and we're going to finish it. But not with three Mini M-16s, that's for damned sure. Let's get back down the side—"

All three of them froze. Someone was approaching: they could hear human sounds even above the rush of the waterfall. Claude poked each of the men once to let them know he'd handle it. He carefully laid his rifle on the ground beside Nile and got up on his haunches. He moved slowly backward, toward the sounds that were still approaching.

Two men were talking loudly to each other in a language that might have been Spanish or Portuguese— Claude wasn't sure, and he wasn't about to undertake a linguistic analysis to find out.

They were deep in a discussion, raising their voices in argument and also to compete with the water. The rocks provided the only possible shelter as there were no bushes large enough to cover a man. Claude thanked God that he and the rest of them had the sense to put on the night cammy. These guards weren't on alert; they weren't expecting any company.

Claude squinted, covering the whites of his eyes, which might have given him away. He slunk back against a large boulder, willing even his chest to limit its movements. The two guards walked right by him, only a couple of feet away. He reached over suddenly with his arms held wide apart. Measuring the distance perfectly, he brought his hands together with a sudden hard movement, as though he were going to theatrically applaud a wonderful performance.

But he had those two heads in between his hands, and the sound that came out wasn't of his clapping, but the sickening and hollow thud of the two skulls coming together, followed almost instantly by the twin sounds of the bone cracking apart. It was one of the simplest but most effective commando techniques known. The human skull, the protector of the brain and all that keeps a man functioning, can be used against him. Break his skull open—or use two skulls to break each other open—and he's gone, as the two guards were.

The two men simply fell to the earth, with the deadweight of dead flesh.

Claude went back and got his rifle. He nodded to the other two, indicating it was all taken care of. Nile went over and crouched by the bodies. "We can't leave them here," he said. "We don't want to leave any calling cards."

"What the hell do you want us to do? They're going to be missed," Liam asked.

"We'll have to carry them down to the beach. We'll strip them, leave their uniforms on the sand, then dump their bodies out at sea. Whoever finds their clothes will get the right idea: they went swimming when they were supposed to be on duty, and they became shark food."

"Damn lot of work to do after I took care of everything else so nice and clean," Claude complained, but even as he did he was handing Liam his Mini M-16 and picking up one of the cadavers to carry it down the steep embankment in a fireman's hold.

Nile did the same, handing Liam his own rifle and taking the other dead man. "Let's get out of here."

"IT'S A SHAME," Liam said to Nile as he watched the second guard's naked body go over the side of the cigar boat. "We might have made use of their uniforms and their weapons. Those Karlsrupas we left on the beach are damn good guns, and so were those Berettas."

"I don't care about the Berettas," Nile said. "I don't take to 9 mm pistols. They're accurate, they're light, and they're easily maintained, but I never trust that they're really going to stop a man. If you hit him anywhere, and its not a mortal wound, you just never know if he's going to get up and keep on coming at you.

"Besides, we couldn't have taken that stuff. The only way those guys' disappearance would ever make sense is if they did do just what we've set up the others to think: go for a swim when they shouldn't, and have something happen to them.

"Anything else would have tipped off the people in charge of that island. I don't know who they are and what they want, and I'm not ready to go in until I find out more. Much more."

Nile looked straight ahead into the night's darkness, and Liam knew better than to say anything more to his boss when the man was in that kind of mood. He left Barrabas to his thoughts.

6

Lee Hatton seldom had the chance to dress up formally. Quite frankly, she liked it quite a bit. She thought of her father for some reason as she walked across the entrance to the French embassy in Matali. She had been the only child of the general and had learned from him all the skills that it took to be one of the SOBs, the elite Soldiers of Barrabas. He had wanted her to have a full life and had encouraged her medical education, not wanting her to be limited by the roles her gender would have assigned to her in the larger society. He would have been delighted to know that she'd moved on into a new life as one of the SOBs, though she thought he'd probably have made some gruff protesting statements about it and the dangers it held for her.

Wouldn't he also have liked her like this, though? she mused.

She was wearing her most elegant gown, a full-length sheath that was made of slinky satin and draped over her body with all the reticence of a body glove. There was no brassiere underneath the dress, and when the ambassador greeted his guests at the door, he seemed unable to lift his eyes above her neck, he was studying the visible thrust of her nipples against the fabric so intently.

"Enchanté," Ambassador de la Garde greeted the couple, who had arranged an invitation for the reception through a bogus introduction to the Matalian minister of finance.

Lee and Geoff spoke in quick French to the ambassador. Their command of Quebecois was part of their cover as the newly married and old-money rich La-Libertés from Montreal, here in Matali to spend their honeymoon and investigate investment possibilities.

Geoff was much less comfortable in his tuxedo than Lee was in her designer gown. Or was it, she wondered, that he was simply uncomfortable with the attention that she was receiving from the other men to whom the ambassador introduced them?

Champagne was being passed around, and they both took glasses while they were introduced to a Herr Groting. "Here from Hamburg," he said, then drank a toast to the couple on hearing that they were newlyweds.

"You're perhaps investigating the region for investments, as well?" Geoff said boldly.

"There's so little worthwhile," the German answered. "I'm more interested in the scenery and the chance to relax."

"I wish my husband could learn to do the same," Lee answered, trying to cover for Geoff's quickness. "It seems I'll have a lot of work to do, taking his mind off his business."

"My dear," Herr Groting responded with a slightly lecherous smile, "if you cannot do that, I shudder for the poor man's future."

"And not mine?" Lee shot back with a smile of her own.

"No, Mrs. LaLiberté, your future is not something I worry about in the least."

Geoff tried to get the conversation back on track. "What is the economic climate here?"

Groting seemed to resign himself to the inevitability of that particular subject. "There's really very little economy that I can see." He was subtly giving in to the pressure and didn't even seem to realize he was contradicting his statement that he wasn't in Matali on business. "The island has few natural resources of value to the West. The agriculture might hold promise, but the farmlands are held in a very strange and inviolate trust by the religious organizations. There isn't private ownership of farmlands as we understand it.

"It's really not unlike your Indians in North America, who thought that the earth was for all of them, as I recall, and who simply didn't understand the idea that a single person, a farmer, could or even would fence off a part of it and claim it for himself.

"The people of the town and the smaller outlying villages simply take from the trees, do some work on the grounds as they feel like it, and that seems to be it." Groting shrugged, dismissing the strange ways of the natives.

"Then fishing?" Geoff continued to press.

Groting's eyes suddenly avoided the younger man's. "Ah, there's the ambassador's wife. Come, you must meet her; she's charming."

Geoff and Lee didn't have time to protest as they were walked across the room to meet the elegant elderly woman who stood by the windows. The fishery issue was obviously a sore point with Groting, Lee saw. She was glad that Nanos was looking into that. There would be something interesting there.

ALEX NANOS WAS ATTENDING his own social event at the moment, though the Dolphin bar and restaurant had little in common with the French embassy.

Nanos was about to polish off a bottle of retsina, his first of the night. The sharp-tasting wine, whose name came from the resin flavoring it, was like mother's milk to Greeks around the world. He'd known he'd end up drinking the stuff as soon as he'd been told that he would be the one to discover what was going on in the port of Matali. Now with Billy Two gone—God knew where—he had to do it by himself.

There were few things to be counted on in this world. One of them had a lot to do with Nanos: wherever there are fishermen, there will be Greeks. There is nothing strange about finding a Greek man in a bar in any harbor in the world. It was in their blood to travel the seas in trade and commerce, and it had been the same for all of history.

Only a few people have spread themselves out over the globe the way the Greeks have. The Jews did, of course, and so did the Lebanese. The Parsis of India went wherever they had to in order to trade. The Arabs did whatever was necessary to spread their Islamic faith. The Greeks? They just seemed to do it because wandering was in their blood, and they only hoped there'd be some fish along the way.

Alex signaled the native bartender for another bottle of the resinated wine. It had been noticeable that no one in the Dolphin bar had even looked twice when the original order had been given. Of course, a waterfront workingman's saloon would carry retsina. It would have to. There would be Greeks coming in to drink as soon as the place opened its doors.

The bottle was plunked down on the table in front of Nanos. When Alex looked up, he didn't see the bartender; what he saw was a vision of his homeland. He squinted a bit to make sure his eyes weren't playing games with him as he studied the dark bearded, heavyset man who now took a chair at his table uninvited.

"On the house," the newcomer announced as he worked the corkscrew into the cork of the bottle of pale rose-colored wine. "And ouzo afterward."

Alex would have groaned if he could at the mention of the potent Greek liqueur. His belly and his head were both going to pay him back for this bit of work tomorrow. It was only five in the afternoon, and he already knew he was going to have the hangover of his life from this assignment.

Well, it was Nile's own fault! he decided as he took the full glass of retsina offered to him. The two men gave each other traditional Greek toasts and downed the wine. The alcohol was already diluting Nanos's blood, and he could feel it making its way into his brain, leaving him with a sensation of light-headedness and the start of being really high.

"You here on the cruise ship?" the newcomer asked. He nodded at the huge white vessel dominating the harbor. It was one of the many liners that plied its trade from one side of the Pacific to the next. It was totally out of scale with the rest of the boats in the harbor.

"Nah. Solo."

Alex introduced himself and got a name back from the other man. "Hank Aggriopolous, from Athens via San Diego." The big guy smiled as they shook hands. "This is my place, my bar."

"Long way from home, whichever one you think is really home," Alex said. He was delighted to see that Hank was going to let him slow down with the booze. They were only sipping now that the first toast had been celebrated with a full glass.

"Athens is my parents' home," Hank announced. "They moved to San Diego during the war, running away from the Nazis." Hank spit on the floor to underline just what he thought about the old German enemies. "I was born there. As American as apple pie, but with a few olives and figs in the middle of it, sort of spicing up the soul." Hank thought the joke was a good one, and his laugh filled up the bar. The regulars were obviously used to hearing him; no one seemed to find anything strange about the outburst.

"So, friend, why are you here, if you're not on the cruise ship?" Hank topped off their wineglasses.

"Just bumming," Alex said, using the perennial excuse of unemployed seamen. No one was ever surprised that a Greek sailor would be between jobs in a foreign port, and no one who understood the life of the sea ever asked the reason for the unemployment. There are many different kinds of honor, and a man's right to privacy was one of the strongest values of the oceangoing world.

"Bad place for that," Hank said, snorting in disgust.

"What do you mean?" Alex looked out over the harbor and pointed to the dozens of fishing trawlers that were in the port. "I broke my teeth on a fishing boat. I thought it'd be a good change of pace to go back to it for a while, especially in a place like this, quiet, out of the way."

Hank's face seemed to cloud over. "There's no work on those boats for a Greek, trust me, friend."

"How come? These Matali natives don't look like the kind of men who'd take to working on a trawler."

"Hell, no, they're just as happy as little clams working their old-fashioned boats, using primitive kinds of nets. There's something going on here, a kind of back-to-the-basics movement that's turning the natives away from anything that has to do with technology.

"They can afford to do that, do without the latest electronics and stuff. The crops and the fish are so plentiful in Matali that there's no need to push nature further than she wants to go. She gives them plenty for the asking.

"They're not the ones taking your job." Hank leaned forward to speak with theatrical confidentiality, even though there was no one close enough to overhear them. "The thing is, there's no *real* fishing being done here. Those boats in the harbor, they're either ones the government confiscated, or they're not really there for fishing.

"Strangest thing I've ever seen, friend. Seems the old man, General Falanu, he wants to scare off the big commercial rigs for some reason.

"The Japanese, the Americans, the Peruvians, all the ones with the big factory boats, they've been told to go away, and if they haven't, the general's creating hell for them. He's got a couple fast corvettes and some observation planes, and he finds them the minute they come inside the two-hundred-mile limit. The next thing they know, they're in a Matali jail and lucky if they get out with their lives. They sure as hell don't get out with their boats."

"Thought you said the natives aren't big on technology," Nanos said as he sipped more of the sharptasting retsina.

"*They* aren't," Hank agreed. "The *general* is. He hires a lot of mercs to play with his gadgets for him."

"Mercs get expensive," Alex said, hoping that his interest wasn't too obvious and trusting that the unspoken bond that is assumed to exist between fellow Greeks was going to forgive him the intimacy of this conversation.

Hank didn't seem to question that. "General's got some money, friend, some very big bucks.

"All I got to tell you is this: you forget a fishing job in Matali, and you forget all those boats out there even exist. Instead—" Hank suddenly sat back in his chair and clapped Alex over the shoulders "—instead you think about drinking ouzo with a countryman.

"Hey, Makan," he called to the bartender, "the ouzo, the real good stuff for my Greek friend. On the house!"

Alex moaned with anticipation.

"HERR GROTING is quite taken with you."

Lee looked over at Geoff Bishop with a smile. "I have many uses in this operation, don't I?" She was playing with him, and with the unusual opportunity to play the vamp.

"Look, keep him occupied. I found out that his house is only a short way from here. He seems a strange one. Maybe there's something to be found by looking around his place. That company he's associated with is one of the big German electronics conglomerates. It seems strange that such a bigwig from there would be headquartered in a place like Matali. I want to find out more."

"There may be a lot to be discovered right here," Lee answered as she saw a rotund man in an overdecorated uniform walk through the doorway. "Unless I'm wrong, that's our General Falanu."

"Great. It means that Groting will stay even longer. You can keep him under your eyes and get to know the general, too. I'll be back in no more than a half hour."

"You're covered, Geoff."

The casual conversation with guests had provided a description of Groting's house, which was like pinpointing it on an island where there weren't that many large residences, and almost all of those were near the

French embassy. In fact, it had seemed that only foreign governments had reason to build showplaces on an island whose simple society wasn't inclined to any ostentation and whose economy hadn't produced any great fortunes.

Geoff left through the formal doors that led to the embassy gardens. He didn't want to draw any attention to himself by leaving through the front of the building, and he also wanted to make sure he had a decent cover for his reentry. He lighted a cigarette outside, so that if anyone was watching him it would appear as though he'd only gone out for a smoke.

He made his way across the back lawn of the embassy and through some shrubs until he came to a street, then made his way southward.

He would have guessed which was Groting's house even if he hadn't had such a good description of it from the gossips at the reception. The guards would have tipped him off.

They weren't in any identifiable military outfit, but there was no question that the men wearing dark berets were uniformed. The three of them wore matching pressed shirts and khaki pants with 9 mm pistols in their holsters beside the sheaths that held their fighting knives. Geoff recognized the handguns as the famous Austrian Steyrs. Whoever was arming the men wasn't stinting on the cost of their hardware. As the trio walked back and forth in front of the entrance to the Victorian-styled house, they each cradled 9 mm Madsen submachine guns in their arms.

The sturdy Danish-made weapon was a favorite of soldiers around the world. Easy to care for, simple to assemble and disassemble, the Madsen had earned its keep in armies from Africa to Asia and most of the rest of the world, as well. Even with the stock extended, the length of the weapon measured only a little more than thirty inches, and its weight was about seven pounds, making it light and quick to aim. It could get off 460 rounds per minute, with great accuracy.

Geoff watched from the shadows to see the pattern of the three men's movements. He quickly saw that he was going to have to take out all of them if he wanted to get into the house. He'd have to do it unarmed, as well. The lightweight tuxedo he wore hadn't provided a way for him to conceal a weapon.

The early evening was quiet; only a few insects buzzed in the background. There was no traffic of any kind in the vicinity right then—neither vehicular or pedestrian. He could move without being noticed.

He solved the problem of his lack of a weapon with a smile. Any soldier worth his salt had to learn to improvise, and Nile Barrabas had certainly made sure his men were all worth at least that much.

Reaching behind himself, he undid the snap on his cummerbund. Although he had always hated the damned things, now the strip of black silk that had covered the waistband of his slacks was proving that it, too, was of a certain value.

He tightened the material into a tight rope by twirling it between his hands. Then he slipped out of the silly patent leather shoes he'd had to wear to the formal occasion and moved in his stocking feet along the unpaved road, staying close to the hedges and using their shadows for camouflage.

At the one moment when he was sure that the three men were as far apart as they could be, he moved quickly, pantherlike, holding up his hands to bring them down in front of the face of the guard closest to him. He jerked the cummerbund back to quickly and savagely cut off the man's air.

The guard was so surprised that he dropped his Madsen. It fell on the lawn, and the grass muffled the sound. Geoff registered the lucky fact that the submachine gun hadn't gone off. He was counting on silence to accompany surprise to let his maneuver work.

It only took a very few quick seconds for Geoff to get his knee up between the guard's shoulder blades. The cummerbund was still cutting into the man's neck, and Geoff quickly jerked his leg and arms in unison, efficiently breaking the man's neck.

The body dropped to the ground. Geoff reached down and grabbed the man's knife from its sheath.

He moved along the hedges and was almost abreast the second guard just when the man turned and saw the corpse. He opened his mouth to shout a warning but Geoff's knife sliced his neck.

The blood gushed from the man's dying body in one forceful spurt, then a second spurt delivered all the heart could pump out before he, too, collapsed to the ground.

The third guard had time to sense more of the danger than the others had. He had no one to yell to, however, and he seemed to know it. But the intruder was yards away from him, and that should allow enough time to find out just how effective the Madsen was. Lifting it up, he sighted along the barrel.

Geoff thanked Billy Two for all the lessons in Osage warrior tactics he'd given the rest of the SOBs. Bishop's hand held the blade of the knife in back of his own head and then threw it with all the force he had toward the alerted guard.

The metal had been kept in good shape. It was fine, hard German steel. It had no problem piercing the guard's skull, just between his eyes. The man froze. Geoff thought for a moment that he would still get off a round from the Madsen, whose barrel was aimed right at his own chest. But the body simply slumped forward onto its knees.

The machine gun propped up the man in his kneeling position for what seemed to be a full and obscene minute. The stock was wedged underneath one of his armpits, the barrel stuck into the earth. But the man finally toppled over onto his side.

The way seemed clear. Geoff wiped the blade on the grass and then made his way up the path. He wasn't going to chance any other guards, though, and rather than go right through the front door, he moved to the side of the house.

Groting evidently trusted his trio of guards enough that he didn't seem to need any more security than them on this island paradise. The windows were open. Geoff was able to climb into one with ease.

He was in a piece of old Germany unbelievably transported to the Pacific. The furniture in the rooms was heavy, dark wood. The carpets were ornate and thick. The paintings on the wall were baroque images that seemed to have little to do with either the modern age or a tropical paradise.

Geoff made his way through the first floor of the house and found more of the same style all through it.

The second floor couldn't have been more different. He stood at the entrance to the first room he came to and studied it in amazement.

It was as loaded with instruments as the tower in a modern airport. There were sensing machines and highly advanced radar. An oversize computer screen was alive with moving characters that would have meant nothing to the unpracticed eye, but Geoff, a highly trained pilot, understood them immediately. They were monitoring all air traffic for hundreds of miles around the island.

What was more interesting were the constants that had been programmed into the computerized charts. Geoff studied them for a while, trying to figure out their meaning. Then it came to him. They were the outlines of a rocket's trajectory, and the point they were coming from was nearby, only a few miles from the main island of Matali.

He had his information. He had to get back to the party and secure his and Lee's cover. He hoped she'd gotten something from him. This guy was more than a little interesting.

"DARLING, HAVE YOU TRIED the buffet? It's wonderful."

"No, I've been—"

"It's obvious what your husband's been up to, Mrs. LaLiberté," Groting said with a smirk on his face.

Geoff turned to face him, hoping his smile was sincere-looking.

"He wasn't satisfied with the champagne with which we mortals have to make do. He has forced the ambassador to open up his justifiably famous wine cellar to bring out some of his prize Bordeaux. The ambassador is always willing to show off," Groting finished as he pointed to the small dots of red that marked Geoff's formal shirt.

Geoff smiled. "I promised the ambassador I wouldn't tell any of the other guests what we were up to. He wasn't quite ready to serve the entire party. You'll keep the secret, won't you, Herr Groting?"

"Of course, young man, of course."

"You should be more careful when you drink red wine, dear. It's difficult to get the stains out, sometimes impossible. And look at the way you've already wrinkled your cummerbund!" Lee said next, impersonating the concerned wife.

"The married life!" Groting exclaimed. "How quickly you'll become accustomed to it."

"Yes, I suppose," Geoff said. He felt a sudden rush of discomfort that was the result of a sense that his real purpose would be immediately exposed, but finally allowed himself to realize that the explanation Groting had offered on his behalf would hold water. How convenient, Geoff thought, because there had been nothing he could have done about the minuscule specks of blood.

ALEX NANOS HAD MEANT his excuse for a change. He really did need to get some air and clear his head.

HIT
THE JACKPOT
WITH GOLD EAGLE

Scratch off the 3 windows
to see what you'll get—FREE!

Then peel off Sticker, affix it to your Scorecard
and mail today to claim your Free Prizes!

IF YOU HIT THE JACKPOT, YOU GET 4 FREE BOOKS AND A FREE POCKETKNIFE

The free gifts shown on the slot machine Sticker are yours to keep forever—even if you never buy another book from Gold Eagle. But wait, there's more...

SCORE A BIGGER BONANZA AS A GOLD EAGLE SUBSCRIBER

Life is a game of chance, but you can be one of its lucky winners. How? By getting the world's hottest action-adventure novels delivered right to your home on a regular basis.

As a Gold Eagle subscriber, you'll rack up an unbeatable combination of benefits and privileges:

- You'll get 6 brand-new titles every second month (2 *Mack Bolans* and one each of *Able Team*, *Phoenix Force*, *Vietnam: Ground Zero* and *SOBs*) hot off the presses—and before they're available in stores.

- You'll save a hefty 12% off the retail price—you pay only $2.49 per book (plus 95¢ postage and handling per shipment).

- You'll get our newsletter, AUTOMAG, *free* with every shipment.

- You'll get special books to preview or purchase at deep discounts.

YOUR NO-RISK GUARANTEE

As a subscriber, you can always cancel, return a shipment and owe nothing—so how can you lose?

RUSH YOUR ORDER TO US TODAY!

Yours FREE—this stainless-steel pocketknife.

Talk about versatile! You get 7 functions in this one handy device—screwdriver, bottle opener, nail cleaner, nail file, knife, scissors and key chain. Perfect for pocket, tool kit, tackle box. And it's yours free if it appears on your slot machine Sticker.

® GOLD EAGLE READER SERVICE
YOUR SCORECARD

Did you hit
the jackpot
with 4 Free
Books
and a Free
Pocketknife?

PEEL OFF STICKER
FROM SLOT MACHINE
AND PLACE IT HERE

☐ **YES!** I hit the jackpot. Please rush me the free gifts on the Sticker that I have affixed above. Then enroll me as a Gold Eagle subscriber with all the benefits and privileges outlined on the opposite page, including a no-risk money-back guarantee if I'm not satisfied.

166 CIM PAMT

Name   (PLEASE PRINT)

Address   Apt.

City

State   Zip

GOOD LUCK

Offer limited to one per household and not valid for
present subscribers. Prices subject to change.

PRINTED IN U.S.A.

Luckily, Hank had been forgiving. The dinner hour was coming up, and crowds were beginning to show up at the Dolphin bar. Besides, he needed time to create the Greek feast he insisted his new friend share with him.

"There'll be stuffed grape leaves, moussaka. The best for my friend from the old country!"

Hank had slapped Alex on the back so hard that the Greek nearly fell flat on his face. His balance was already seriously impaired by the retsina and the ouzo.

Alex was delighted to get outdoors, and he made his way to the harborside beach where Hank had assured him the locals swam. Alex got there, though his path was a little crooked. He stood by the water and looked out at the fishing fleet that was assembled there.

A group of youngsters came running up to the water with disgusting energy and very loud yells that sounded horrible to Alex's tender ears and mind. They raced by him to jump directly into the Pacific, splashing him with the warm water, even though their approach to the dives had been nearly professional in execution and they'd entered the water cleanly.

Alex was in such bad shape that he didn't actually register for a full beat of time the fact that all of the group of six or seven were naked. The lot of them were yelling and screaming, playfully splashing water at one another.

If skinny-dipping was the norm in the place, Alex wasn't going to argue and insist on regulation bathing trunks. He just wanted to get in the water himself and hope that it would help with the overdose of alcohol sloshing in his skull.

He stripped down to his underwear, dropping his clothes on the sand. Then he ran into the harbor water all at once, as though he couldn't wait to submerge his feverish flesh.

The embracing ocean seemed to soothe him immediately. He opened his eyes and saw the purity of the stuff. There was no pollution on Matali. He could see many feet down to the bottom of the harbor with almost as much clarity as sighting the mountain peaks of the island itself on a clear day.

There was something wonderful about the pure state of nature. Just the perception of it made Alex feel much better physically. The water was smooth-feeling, and the salty taste of the ocean would perhaps be a preventive antidote to the pounding in his head that, while not yet present, he had been preparing himself for since the first draft of retsina.

Nanos came up to the surface and began to swim out into the harbor. He heard some shouts from the kids and thought they might be trying to warn him off, but the sounds ebbed away. He was the strongest swimmer in the SOBs. His training as a frogman had only intensified his natural ability. His well-trained body was fighting off the effects of the retsina and the ouzo, and he had no problem keeping up a steady Australian crawl.

He was heading toward one of the boats. He didn't care which one he hit first; he just wanted to check them out a little bit, and the cover of ignorance was one of the best that he had at the moment. He was just a dumb Greek sailor who'd had too much to drink and who was about to swim offshore too far.

"Hey! You!" The voice that finally called out to him lilted with the accents of the American South. Alex stopped his stroke and began to tread water. He exaggerated the heaviness of his breathing, hoping to convince whoever had hailed him that he was much more winded than he actually was.

"Man, where are you from?" Alex asked, slurring his words.

"Hell, man, you're whacked out." The guard on the fishing boat Alex had swum up to was buying the entire act.

"Come on up here, boy, and get yourself a rest."

The man was overweight, but Alex could see that the big belly hid a considerable mass of strength. It wasn't one of those flabby ones. Alex allowed himself to be heaved over the side of the boat.

"Damn, you're drunk like a skunk, too," the man laughed. "Hey, Joe Bob, come see this."

Another man came up out of the cabin. "For Christ's sake, Jimmy, no one's supposed to come up onto the boats!"

"Hey, Joe Bob, this fella speaks American. He jus' had a little too much to drink. The only neighborly thing to do is help him get some breath and then give him some more."

"If the general finds out, he's gonna have your balls, Jimmy."

"Nah." The one with the belly grinned at Alex as he handed him a towel to dry off with. "And put it 'round your belly to cover yourself, too.

"Come on, Joe Bob. Break out the Jim Beam for our friend."

The one who scowled and went downstairs was much more bothersome than the first cracker, Alex thought, recognizing the danger at once. Joe Bob was slender and hard and had a mean look on his face that Nanos just knew was a permanent fixture. But Alex was getting just what he needed and wanted, a tour of one of the boats.

As soon as Hank had told him that there was something about the fishing fleet that made it off limits for a Greek sailor, Alex had known that he had to check out the situation and get word back to Nile. There was definitely something of interest going on.

Joe Bob did come back up with the promised bottle of bourbon, carrying a plastic bag of ice in his other hand. There were already plastic glasses scattered about on the deck of the boat.

"Now we can have us a party, just like home!" Jimmy opened the bottle and poured out hefty doses of bourbon for all three of them. Joe Bob put ice in the glasses and then emptied the bag into a cooler that was on the deck.

To Alex's amazement, to his utter astonishment, Joe Bob then threw the plastic bag over the side, into the harbor. He watched that and remembered the purity of the ocean when he'd dived under its surface. Suddenly his mind was full of images of the waste-ridden beaches of America and Europe. He remembered the stench of the Bay of Naples, where the entire metropolitan area's untreated garbage and sewage was pumped into waters that poets had once proclaimed the most beautiful in the world. He had visions of the expanses of barrier beaches on the eastern seaboard, hundreds of miles, from Cape Hatteras to Cape Cod, covered with empty beer bottles and Twinkie wrappers.

Alex looked at Joe Bob and saw evil.

"You guys have a nice boat here," Alex said, forcing himself back to the situation at hand.

"Hell, boring, that's what it is," Jimmy sneered. "No fun, not at all. And those natives are as lazy as niggers. I tell you, no American should be stuck out here so far from white wenches the way we are."

Joe Bob was looking out over the rest of the harbor. Alex thought about his friend Claude Hayes and the heroism the black man had performed in their years together in the SOBs. The idea that anyone as scuzzy-looking as Jimmy would dare talk that way began to get under his skin.

Joe Bob reached to his waist and pulled on the bottom of his T-shirt, lifting it up over his head. His torso was covered with crude tattoos, most of them advertising slogans with lurid flourishes.

One, across his right biceps, caught Alex's attention. It read, White Power.

Oh, yeah? Alex thought with a sneer.

"What you guys doing here, anyway?" Alex asked aloud casually, finally getting his question out. "You fishermen?"

"Nah," Jimmy answered, patting his substantial stomach. "Just some guys on a job."

Joe Bob snorted in agreement.

"I gotta use your head," Alex said. It was time to find out what else was going on here. He wanted to take a look around before he got too angry with these ignoramuses and their prejudices, or before the alcohol brought out his own mean streak.

He moved toward the entry to the boat's cabin.

"Don't go in there!" Joe Bob shouted at him.

Alex turned around to look at the other American. "Something wrong? I just gotta go."

"We can't let anyone—"

"For golly's sake, Joe Bob, the man's a friend drinking our bourbon with us. Let him go take a whiz."

"Jimmy, you know the orders. No one's supposed to go inside the cabin."

"Go on." Jimmy waved to Alex. "I'll take care of this."

Alex walked down the short, steep stairwell into the cabin. The head was clearly marked at the bottom of the stairs, but the conversation had made Nanos all the more interested in the trawler.

He opened and shut the door loudly, just in case Joe Bob was monitoring the sounds he was making. Then he moved swiftly and quietly down the hallway, trying to scan the insides of the various cabins along the corridor.

The first two were obviously the men's living quarters. One was plastered with posters of naked women that suggested the occupant fed his hunger by continuously being reminded what he was missing. The other was simply messy, with piles of junk food wrappers cluttering up the floor.

Alex couldn't figure out which cabin was whose. They both fit the two men he assumed were mercenaries.

The last cubbyhole along on the corridor was the jackpot, one bigger than he'd ever expected to find. The place was crammed with state-of-the-art electronic equipment. He could barely identify what it was; it would take someone with Nate's electronic ability to figure out what were all the gadgets in the small space.

One thing was for sure; the trawler wasn't a simple fishing boat. Hank had been right.

Alex backed out of the cabin and shut the door. When he turned to go back to the head, he found Joe Bob standing there waiting for him. In his hand was a bowie knife. The sharp, thick blade was highly polished, catching the slightest reflection from the bare bulb that lit the passageway.

"We told you not to do nothin' but go to the head."

"No, you didn't," Alex said. "Hey, man, I was just taking a look—"

He didn't have a chance to finish the sentence as Joe Bob lunged at him. Alex's training made him react, moving instinctively to avoid the frontal attack. He didn't let that keep him from countering it with his own automatic reflex.

Joe Bob's assault had been ill-timed and made with the overconfidence of a man who was used to getting his way physically. He'd assumed the knife point would find its mark and end the argument there and then. But Alex's ability to avoid the blade threw Joe Bob off balance.

The other man kept moving forward. Even then Joe Bob would have regained himself if his opponent hadn't been one of the SOBs.

Alex, without thinking, brought the side of his right palm down on the man's outstretched arm. The blunt instrument that was Nanos's hand cracked against the man's forearm. There was the unmistakable sound of bone breaking. Joe Bob was in too much pain for that split second to even get a scream out of his throat.

He didn't have more than that second for another try. Alex's arm lifted up once more, and this time, when it came crashing down, it landed on the back of the man's neck. The same soft and final sound of breakage was the result, and Joe Bob fell to the deck, silent and dead.

The knife he'd been holding clattered along the deck's wooden surface. "Hey, what's goin' on down there?" It was the echoing sound of the knife that had attracted Jimmy's attention.

Alex quickly tried to move the body into one of the cabins before Jimmy decided to come and take a look, but there wasn't time.

"Nothing, man," Alex yelled back up to the outer deck. "Everything's fine."

Alex let the body slide to the floor. Then he left it and went up the stairs to find Jimmy still holding a glass of his bourbon.

"Got a fresh one for me?" Alex said as he sat down in the deck chair beside the fat man.

"Sure, buddy," Jimmy answered, but he seemed worried. "Where's Joe Bob?"

"He had to use the head after me," Alex said as he took the newly filled glass from Jimmy.

Jimmy was more puzzled and seemed to become suddenly more suspicious. "Think I better check on him.'' He stood up and started to move toward the stairs.

''What's the matter, you don't think he knows how to find his own way back?'' Alex joked.

Jimmy wasn't buying any. He looked at Alex and put his hand on his pistol, as if to reassure himself it was still there. Then he turned once more.

Alex knew he couldn't let the man go down there, but he was in his briefs and unarmed himself. He looked around quickly and tried to gauge the situation and the possibilities. The stairs were on the port side of the boat. The rest of the ersatz fishing fleet was anchoring to the lee. No one else would see them from the stairway. He decided it was time for Jimmy to go for a swim.

He was able to get a couple of good strides on the bigger man before his own flying body slammed into Jimmy's. The fat man was right at the top of the stairway, only a few feet from the guardrail that protected the afterdeck of the fishing boat. The momentum of Alex's unexpected attack forced the two of them, automatically grappling with each other, over the side. They went into the water with a big splash.

The two men went under at once. The surprise had given Alex the advantage, and Jimmy was also a much less talented swimmer. The big man made the first mistake to be made in a situation like that one, and he began to struggle madly to get to the surface and the air that he knew was there. He wasn't paying any attention to the more immediate problem of Nanos.

Alex had taken a good breath before they'd gone under. He had more strength underwater where Jimmy's greater bulk wasn't going to help. He didn't even really have to do that much to finish the quick battle.

He grabbed Jimmy by the neck and pulled downward, giving the other man the impression that he was going to keep him from the air—which was precisely what Nanos intended to do—and making him become even more panicky.

Once the real panic set in, Jimmy was lost. He opened his mouth, but only water rushed into his lungs. Violently thrashing about with his legs, he was expending energy he should have retained for other purposes. He began to try to deliver a hard fist at Nanos, not realizing that the water would blunt its impact.

Alex pressed harder on the other man's neck. He ignored the muffled kicks and hits that were coming. Using his legs to propel him up over Jimmy, the Greek kept his body between the other man and the air he was becoming all the more desperate to reach.

Suddenly Jimmy gave up. His eyes bulged obscenely as he realized that he wasn't going to make it. His mouth opened one last time in what must have been a scream of death, and a huge bubble of air came from his protesting lungs. Then he went limp.

Alex let go then and drifted to the top. When he broke the surface of the water, he let his own mouth open wide to accept into his lungs the life-giving oxygen.

The clear waters and the wide arc of the sky above seemed even more beautiful than before as Nanos relished the simple act of breathing.

He had to get to shore. He began a slow crawl, not back up to his full capacity yet. As he moved away from the fishing boat, Jimmy's body broke the surface, though only his shoulder blades showed. Alex didn't think the body would be noticed while he was still near the boat. It was time to get back to the island and let Nile and the rest of the team know what he'd found out. Before he let his thoughts go blank with the monotonous rhythm of swimming, Nanos wondered what Billy Two was doing.

7

Billy Two was horrified when he discovered that the old priest had no name.

"We who are the priests of Matali deserve no name," the old man told him. "We cannot name ourselves until the god is satisfied."

If he'd never known how important that particular mission of his was before, Billy Two understood as soon as the priest explained that to him.

"It's not just that we sent the god away," the priest continued, "it's that we have defiled his temple."

"*You* didn't do it!" Billy Two insisted.

"But we allowed others to." The priest was contemplative in the dawn light. "We must carry the responsibility. We are also responsible for the ways that things have happened in Matali. We have not shown the people the true way."

The priest hung his head in unhappiness after his admission. "We thought that the Westerners were harmless for many, many years. Then they fought their great war with the Japanese and they brought their sick and wounded here to be healed. We thought that was honorable, and even we, the priests, tried to help.

"We lived on the god's island then, the one they call Devil's Land now, in their foolishness. Or perhaps it's not foolish. If the god is not in his place, then the devil must be there, I suppose.

"We let the Westerners take the island and turn it into a hospital. We all volunteered then to help nurse them and to pray for them.

"They were saving us from the Japanese, and they were acting in the honorable traditions of warriors by doing so, we thought.

"Once they were there, the governments wouldn't leave. We tried to ignore the new regime and the foolish General Falanu, who would like to think he is one of the Westerners. We still counter him in the lives and the hearts of the people, but we were forced to leave the god's island and he took over. He invited in the other Westerners who have defiled the holy land."

The priest, like so many others in countries other than North America and Europe, couldn't distinguish between the nationalities of whites. They were simply "the Westerners" to him.

"I will save the island, and you can take a name." Billy Two thought of the enormity of the situation: to not have a name! To a European, it would seem simply a strange thing, but to a man of his heritage it meant that his soul had no mooring. A male is named by his father and, in the process of being named, is brought into the cycle of life, given his history, and begins to live out his destiny.

"Yes, my son, you will. It is in the promises of our ancestors. But you must do it by the law of the god."

Billy Two looked at the old man and waited.

"You must not use the Westerner's arms against him. You must enter the battle as a warrior of the god. You must follow his dictates."

"What are they?"

"You may only fight with what you construct yourself. You must make your own boat to go to the island and carry only weapons that you can make with your own hands and your own skill. You may wear only articles of clothing that you make yourself. You must be blessed in our ceremony, and all your weapons and clothing with you. Then you must go alone, across the water, to the island, and you must meet the forces of evil. If your soul has been pure, you will be victorious."

"But, father, what if I am impure?" Billy Two thought back to his father's house in Oklahoma and all the processed foods and processed ideas that he'd been fed there. How far from the way of the Osage had he gone?

The old man didn't answer with a word, but only put a hand on Billy Two's shoulder and gripped it hard. The Osage understood the response. There was no way to be sure. He would only find out in battle itself.

The man got up then and went to the front of the temple where they'd been sitting. He began to chant the morning rituals in front of the altar of the god he believed in.

On the altar was another statue like the one before the temple's entrance. It, too, was the image of Hawk Spirit that had come to Billy Two so often in the years since his incarceration in the Soviet prison. He studied it carefully from his seat, still unable to get over the likeness between the image and the spirit that had been visiting him so regularly.

The priest's voice began a new and louder chant, and Billy Two suddenly sat bolt upright. He knew that sound! He remembered dimly his grandfathers, men who had kept the ways of the Osage that his father had abandoned, and he recalled them singing to him when he was barely more than an infant.

It had been this song!

Billy Two stood up and stormed to the front of the temple. He interrupted the priest, not able to wait until the end of the ceremony. "What is that? What are you chanting?"

The old man seemed slightly embarrassed by the question. "Forgive me. I felt, for a while, that you were like a young boy, one who has only begun his journey in life. I was praying to the god to look over the newborn infant. I don't know what possessed me to say that particular prayer.

"It's one that's usually said by uncles and grandfathers when they visit with the newborn males of their clans."

Billy Two felt a wave of some strange emotion sweep over his body. The temple was suddenly too close, too confining. He turned around and walked quickly outdoors. He was confronted with the statue of his Hawk Spirit; the one outside the temple was much larger than the image on the altar.

Billy Two tried to grasp what he had learned in school all his life. His mind worked overtime to remember all the anthropological explanations—the migrations of ancient peoples, the way that some concepts reappear in the world's religions over and over again in remarkably similar form.

It was only coincidence that such songs would be the same here on Matali and in his grandfathers' houses in Oklahoma. It was only his damaged mind that made him think he was actually encountering his Hawk Spirit. There could be no other explanation. He needed help. He should stop all of this and go to Lee Hatton and ask her—

I have many lives and many forms and many peoples.... The wings of Hawk Spirit span the world and beyond it....

The words he'd heard in the Sierras reverberated in Billy Two's mind, as though they were being freshly spoken there, at that moment, as though Hawk Spirit was responding to his doubt.

"What the hell have I gotten into?" Billy Two asked himself out loud. "How can I fight this?"

He stood there for a while and then realized he was sweating profusely. The tension had gotten to him, he supposed. The whole situation was getting to him in many different ways.

Then, suddenly, his muscles relaxed, and he realized his own answers. "I won't fight it. There is no way to fight it. There is no reason to fight it."

The priest was standing by him then. Billy Two turned toward him with full trust. "I need tender young birch to make my bows and arrows, but I don't think you have trees called that on this island. Walk in the forests with me, and we'll see what there is here. I have to begin to prepare myself."

The priest looked up at Billy Two and smiled. "Of course you will. I have always known you would."

"WHAT HAVE YOU and Billy Two come up with?" The voice of Nile Barrabas seemed to blow apart Alex's head.

Where was he? *Matali!* That was it!

Then he remembered the last of the night before— or at least his stomach did. It rebelled at the memory of the rich Greek food and the endless glasses of retsina and ouzo.

His brain unwillingly entered the action as well, performing its own insurrection. The memory of the battle on the boat in the harbor jolted him into sudden alertness.

"Nile," Alex spoke into the microwave set that was his means of communication with the SOBs' headquarters on the private resort island, "there's a whole lot of strange stuff coming down here. I got on one of the vessels in the harbor. They look like fishing trawlers, but they sure as hell aren't. They have enough computer gear to make Beck happy for the rest of his life. He can move here from Olde Lyme and never miss a beat."

"Hell he can. Damn, Nanos, nothing on these islands is what it appears to be. Fishing boats are high-tech and abandoned islands are missile sites.

"You and Billy Two keep it up. I'll want more on these boats."

"Um, Nile, I don't know.... I don't know where Billy Two is. He sort of disappeared yesterday, and I haven't seen him since."

There was a moment of silence on the other end of the scrambled microwave transmission. None of the SOBs was supposed to be an independent. The report that one of them was unaccounted for meant only one thing to Nile, and his response expressed it. "He must be in trouble. You'll have to find him."

"Nile, I don't think—" Alex was having a hard time voicing what he had to say, not only because of his ungodly hangover but also because he was worried about Billy Two and about what the leader of the team would think about his departure.

But in the end there was only one way to handle that kind of situation in the field: tell the truth and get it out. In the context of the military discipline with which the SOBs had to operate, hiding the problems or mistakes of a fellow soldier was as bad as or even worse than the original offense.

"Look, Nile, I think Billy Two's losing it. It's been coming up, and I've talked to Lee about it. It's him and his Hawk Spirit thing, you know? I think Billy Two's off meditating or speaking in tongues or doing whatever the Osages do when they go off the deep end. I don't understand this stuff, Nile, I really don't. I just don't think this means that Billy Two's in trouble in the usual way. I don't think we need to spend time going after him right now.

"I'll talk to Lee about it," Nanos offered finally.

"Hell you will," Barrabas answered curtly over the microwave. "She has more than enough of her own work to do. We'll deal with it when this is all over. Damn, Nanos, how did I let this happen?"

"Don't blame yourself, Nile. I reported this to Lee, and even she didn't think there was an immediate problem."

"Fine. Enough of this. I actually saw some of it coming. Alex, keep up with your assignment. We need to know more about those damn boats. You also better figure out a means to neutralize them if it comes to that, and it probably will.

"Forget Billy Two, and don't bother Lee and Geoff about it. Let them focus on what they have going on their own."

"You got it, Nile," Alex said gratefully. The line went dead then. Nanos stood up. His movement was too quick, and the pounding in his head increased in speed and intensity all of a sudden. He sat down again and damned the person who thought of making retsina in the first place, and then found some choice swear words for Billy Two's parents, as well. Somehow, in his state, it seemed it must all be their fault.

When he got his bearings back and thought that it might be possible to attempt to stand once more—if he made it a much slower attempt—Alex discovered that he had a different take on the whole thing, one less impersonal.

What would Nile really think of the situation? Would he boot Billy Two off the team? The Osage was Alex's best friend, and no matter how much a fellow talks about liking everyone in a group like the SOBs— and Nanos did like them all—he just doesn't forsake a friend like that, not after everything Billy Two and Alex had been through together.

Just how much trouble was Billy Two in? Just how far over the line had the man gone? Could he ever function as one of the SOBs again?

Alex's head began to throb with even more pain than before. He was getting into a world-class headache of an assignment.

"ALL OF THIS is such a pleasant addition to our honeymoon, General Falanu," Lee Hatton said with a charming smile. She was dressed in a loose skirt that contrasted with the fit of her very tight blouse.

The corpulent general appreciated his guest's shapely attributes as he held out his hand to help her climb down the gangplank onto his presidential yacht. "It is a great pleasure for us to entertain such an elegant woman."

Geoff followed Lee onto the yacht and took one of the cushioned seats beside her, on the other side of the general who'd made the offer of the private cruise at the French ambassador's reception the previous night. Lee had used all her cunning on the man after he'd arrived. She'd been the personification of poise and good breeding.

She'd been a goddamn belle of the ball, Geoff thought to himself. He wasn't used to seeing Lee in that role. She was much more comfortable for him to deal with when they were alone at one of their homes or with the rest of the team, where Lee was a full member and so competent on the field and valuable as a compatriot that they were all in danger of forgetting her feminine qualities. Geoff felt he was learning some lessons about that side of Lee during the mission. He wouldn't forget them soon, he promised himself.

The yacht's motor began to purr as soon as they were served their cocktails and the general had signaled the captain with his hand.

"You've worked hard to make Matali a modern state, I understand," Lee began, trying to draw the general out in conversation. "I hear you've been quite successful."

The general's disposition took a turn toward sourness. "There are many roadblocks to that, I'm afraid. The religion of the common people is the major one. We're burdened with all of the weight of ignorance one can imagine. I seldom agree with the Communists, but my experience with the priests of Matali makes me think they were right when they called religion the opiate of the masses."

The subject was a sore one, no doubt about it.

The boat picked up speed after it left the confines of the main harbor of Matali. They were following in the wake of the large cruise ship that had been in port to dump hundreds of free-spending tourists into the town in the past few days.

"It's commerce such as that which will really make Matali modern," the general said as he pointed to the huge hull of the ship ahead of them.

Lee looked at it and shuddered internally. She'd watched the tourists disrupt the small city with their demands and bad manners, and she hardly wanted to equate the hordes of loudmouthed vacationers with progress.

The general began to reel off the profit figures involved with the visit of one of those cruise liners. Geoff, acting the role of the potential investor, leaned over to show more interest in what the fat man was saying.

"There was talk that the tourists caused some problems in the town, though," Geoff mentioned.

Falanu's expression became darker. "There were some unfortunate disturbances that must have come from them." The way he spoke betrayed his disbelief.

"Certainly it couldn't come from the natives: they're so nonaggressive, it seems," Geoff remarked, pressing home his point. "Your priests whom you dislike so much are pacifists, I'm told."

"Yes, yes, they are," Falanu said softly, as though he was weighing the same facts in his own mind.

"Enough of this!" he exclaimed jovially, suddenly changing the topic and grabbing hold of Lee's hand. "I am going to show you the most amazing part of Matali, the one thing that is the most interesting of all. It is supposed to be a secret. No one is to know of it. I will use my great influence to let you share in it, though."

"I can't wait!" Lee said, speaking just as theatrically as the dictator. She looked at Geoff, and a fleeting silent communication passed between them. Was the man really going to let them have an inside look at the space island? Could their luck be that good?

In a while, it became obvious that it wasn't. They were, in fact, coming up to an island, but it wasn't Devil's Land. It was the resort island where the rest of the team was waiting for action.

As soon as Lee understood, she turned once more to Geoff to try to see what he thought they should do. She'd been enduring the dictator's endlessly boring conversation for the whole journey across the Pacific. She thought that his lack of intelligence and grace would be enough in itself to drive her to action. The idea that he might be uncovering the SOBs' base was an almost unnecessary corollary motivation.

"There!" The general pointed to a single-story house that was visible beyond the bright white beach. He gave the actor's name with evident pride. "We're lucky to have such a man here. We hope to use his name to promote the island for the tourists. There will be many more cruise ships coming to port if the visitors think that they're sharing something with such a big star."

Lee tensed. If the yacht got any closer to the shore, she and Geoff would have to be ready to act. They couldn't allow the entire operation to be uncovered in this mindless fashion.

She looked at the Kevlar cigar boat tied to the dock near the structure. She could see the revolving screens sticking up from the fireplace chimneys. Obviously, anyone with any military training would have to know what that was about.

Geoff had to have the same thoughts. She saw him stand and move toward the cabin of the yacht to check out the captain and the general's bodyguards. He was wondering just how dangerous they were going to be. The two SOBs were unarmed. The bodyguards were all equipped with pistols, at least, and there were probably carbines and possibly even automatic weapons on board the dictator's private boat.

"I'm afraid we'll have to turn back now," the general said with a smile. "We've promised our actor friend complete privacy for the time being, and until the opportunity is ripe for the greatest possible amount of publicity, I intend to respect it.

"Besides, you people must be ready for lunch now. I know how the ocean feeds the appetite!" He pounded his substantial belly, then shouted an order to the captain.

The yacht turned sharply and appeared to head back to Matali.

Lee was stunned. She'd been ready for action, and now there was no need for any. She looked at the dictator for a moment and finally asked him, "General, what did you study at West Point?"

The general blushed. "Well, I had an interesting time there, of course." Then he went on to discuss the plans for the garden party lunch they were going to attend at his mansion.

Lee understood immediately that the man had never gotten a real West Point degree. They had expected to deal with a real military adversary, but that wasn't the case. The man was a fake soldier, one of those the State Department forces on the military academies as a matter of foreign policy.

She looked over at the bodyguards and wondered if they were more dangerous or if they were as harmless as the general—or rather, she corrected herself, as inept. When she caught the look of one of them, one who appeared to be the most senior, she was glad she hadn't let her surveillance down too completely. He was turned toward the private island, studying something with an intent look, and there was little doubt in her mind that it was the revolving screens Nate Beck had constructed for the SOBs' communications and the observation of the space island.

The dictator might be a fool, but there were some real dangers in the operation yet, there was no doubt about it.

NILE BARRABAS WALKED OUT from the house only when the visiting yacht had become a tiny speck on the horizon. He hadn't been about to take the chance of being seen and identified by the intruding vessel.

As soon as the white-haired leader of the SOBs was standing on the patio of the house, the three other men came out from their own hiding places to join him.

"Did you see who that was?" Nate asked excitedly.

"Yeah," Nile answered. "Hell of a story behind that one, I bet."

"If Lee and Geoff had had any idea about it, they would have warned us," Claude Hayes said evenly. He obviously wasn't going to let the incident freak him. "There's a good reason for it."

"We'll get a report from them later, for sure," Nile said. "I have to get on the horn to the Fixer. Jessup sure as hell has a lot to answer for, getting us into this one. We don't have anything close to the level of arms we need to handle the situation."

"We could get some from the island, I bet," Liam said. Having grown up in Ireland, and having fought for the IRA, O'Toole was used to scrounging up his own arsenals. He hadn't gotten his start in that kind of life by having access to unlimited hardware.

"We don't even know what the hell is over there!" Nile said, suddenly angrier. "We saw the missiles, sure. So they have the capability of an air defense. We also saw a hell of a lot of armed men."

"At least one hundred," Claude added.

"Quite possibly more," Nile said back to him. "We don't have a clue what kind of shape they're in, what kind of training they've had. I'll lead you men just about anywhere against just about any foe. You've proven yourselves over and over again, and I have no reason to think there's any army on the face of the earth that could stand up to you. But I won't take you on a suicide mission, and this may be as close as we've ever gotten to that in our career together.

"Jessup's going to have to come up with some heavy stuff for us to use before we take on the forces on that island. He's halfway around the globe from us, but he's got his ways of doing it.

"In the meantime, we'll continue to gather intelligence from our people in the field.

"When the time comes to act, we'll be ready."

But the three others who were looking at the man's face knew the idea of lingering there any longer was eating at him. Nile Barrabas was a man of action. Waiting never had been his strong card.

8

"What a pleasure to find such learned company," Lee said to the scientist who sat beside her at the state dinner. "I had no idea someone with your reputation would be here in the South Pacific."

Professor Gasteau seemed strangely ill at ease with the praise. "I'm even more surprised to find myself recognized."

"But, Dr. Gasteau, your studies in aerodynamic design are hardly secrets, especially not to anyone who knows anything about flight. My husband's a pilot, and I long ago learned that I was going to have to be conversant in his interests if our marriage was going to be at all pleasant."

"Oh, yes," Gasteau agreed, although it was evident he still didn't like the explanation. "I am here, actually, on a working holiday. I'm not here in the capital often. I have few reasons to come to the main island. I prefer to spend my time in seclusion on one of the off islands." He tried to gain the upper hand in the conversation. "Though of course I'm delighted to have your companionship. Such a stellar surprise."

"Well! From you, the use of the adjective 'stellar' is really something of an honor," Lee shot back. "On vacation on one of the other islands? Are you staying with the movie star, then? General Falanu has told me about his estate. In fact, though I don't think he was supposed to, the general took us near there in his yacht the other day."

"I am hardly in the arms of luxury, *madame*. In fact, my stay here is strictly professional. I'm afraid that when I used the term 'working vacation,' working should have been the dominant part of the phrase."

"Well, I only hope that the star will arrive while we're still here. I'd love to be able to go back to Montreal and report on his private life. He's said to be terribly scandalous."

"Yes," Gasteau said distractedly, "I hear the same thing. Canada, you say? You're here for only a short while, then?"

"I had thought so. This was meant to be a honeymoon. I'm learning the truth about this husband of mine, though. Everything is an excuse to work. He's been pestering Herr Groting and the general about investment possibilities ever since we got off our plane."

"I wonder what he's interested in on such a place as Matali?" Gasteau said. "Surely there are more promising arenas for his money than this small and primitive island."

"Yes, I'm sure you're right. The difference is, Doctor, that he's *here*. My husband is a workaholic; I'm sure you're familiar with that type of personality. He's convinced there is business to be done, somehow, and he's determined to discover how it is. I think that Geoff treats it all as though it were one big parlor game. There are clues to be found everywhere, he says, and one only has to put together the right pieces to win the prize.''

While she kept up the conversation, Gasteau studied Lee. She maintained her dazzling smile and her constant flow of meaningless monologue to convince him that she was utterly harmless. There seemed to be some point in the conversation when he finally decided that she was simply a very attractive society lady from Canada who was bemused by her husband's constant search for more money.

Once that decision had been made, Gasteau finally relaxed and, in the manner of a true Frenchman, began a barely concealed seduction of her.

She gave back as good as she got, never letting a single innuendo go without response, using her eyes to communicate even more explicit messages to the French scientist.

''If you are so entranced with islands, then there are some others in the archipelago that you must see. The only real farming done around here is on Sakanto, about a hundred miles away. There the natives don't have it quite so easy. The fruit trees and wild game that feed the populace of Matali aren't as plentiful, and they farm more on Sakanto to make up for the difference.''

''Really. My husband will be interested. He was disappointed to learn about the strange land ownership habits of Matali. There had been some talk about pineapple plantations at one point—a big thing in the future, he's convinced—but that seems impossible the way this island is set up. Of course, the Americans have Hawaii tied up already, so we Canadians must look elsewhere for our own possibilities, unless we want to be forever doomed to buying from the United States corporations.''

"Yes." Gasteau's complexion turned darker, as though she'd reminded him of some past wrong a villain had done to him. "One must learn to do without the Americans at all cost."

"Is it difficult not being American or Russian and being so involved in space exploration, Professor? I would think that even the Sorbonne would have limited research possibilities, at least in comparison to what the Pentagon and the Kremlin could offer a man of your caliber."

"Bah! The Ariane is at least as good as anything the superpowers can come up with. We can at least get it off the ground!"

"Oh, yes, the missile your government and the other European countries developed together, the one that's based in Africa."

"Yes." Now Gasteau was being taken off to a more sentimental memory, leaving behind whatever it was that had angered him earlier. "The Ariane is one of the great achievements of the European Community. But our governments have learned too much from the damned Americans.

"They've limited themselves too greatly, assuming that the superpowers will dominate space, certainly in military areas. They have intolerable red tape. They're constantly worried about the idea of a—"

Gasteau was silenced at the crucial moment by the entrance of the liveried servants who were bringing the main course into the dining room. "Ah, the entrée,"

Gasteau said, smiling. "Really, *madame*, the food from the general's kitchen is a much more enticing topic of conversation for someone as beautiful as you. I've bored you with my talk about governments and space. Forgive me.

"Let us instead wonder about the perfection of the *Veau Oscar* the chef has made his specialty. When the general wants us to grace his table and he senses any hesitation on our part to come, he has only to promise this delicacy, and I am on my boat, ready to beg for entrance.

"And besides, you must tell me who is your couturier. Your dress is a work of art." Gasteau smiled as he looked down into Lee's décolletage, obviously more interested in her own natural design than that of her obscuring dress.

Lee had to work hard to force a smile in return. She was seething inside. The man had been about to tell her things she was sure were important, but the moment had been lost.

She picked up her utensils and began to gently slice into her veal, willing herself to maintain her facade of civility.

BILLY TWO WAS EATING his own dinner. His feast had little resemblance to the gold-plated knives and forks of the presidential palace.

He was tearing the roasted meat from a boar's carcass. He brought a handful of the flesh to his mouth, and the fat dripped out through his fingers and trailed down his forearm. He bit off a big chunk of the pork and tasted its gamy flavor.

The rest of the boar's meat was still on the spit over the fire he'd made. He had caught the beast himself, with his own hands, using only a sharpened piece of rock for a weapon.

The animal had made a righteous battle for its life, trying desperately to get its deadly tusks turned in a direction from which it could have repulsed the human's attack. Billy Two had come up behind it, mindful of the wind directions, making sure that the wild pig wouldn't be warned by his odor. He'd actually jumped on the boar's back and had nearly been killed when it had begun to run through the underbrush.

If he'd fallen off before he had killed the boar, Billy Two was sure he would be dead. The animal had outweighed him by at least two hundred pounds. Its sharp hooves could have stomped the life out of him easily.

It hadn't happened that way. The sharp-edged stone had proven to be a fine instrument, and Billy Two had broken open the boar's stomach and then its head with his repeated blows. The animal had collapsed onto the ground afterward, snorting out its last breath before dying.

Billy Two had brought its carcass back to his campsite and had methodically prepared the animal. Its skin was stretched out on a wooden frame nearby. It would answer the priest's demand that Billy Two produce his own clothing and weapons. The meat, most of which was still over the fire, spitting fat onto the hot coals, would give him sustenance for the rest of his journey, along with the fruit that was so plentiful on the island.

The boar's tusks were a real prize. Billy Two was holding two of them in his hands. They were long, sharp, curved pieces of bone that would have a real utility in the coming days. Weapons could be fashioned from the animal's ribs, as well, Billy Two thought with satisfaction.

Following the ways of his ancestors, Billy Two thanked the boar for having lived to such a fine old age and providing the Osage with invaluable assets because of that. A younger, smaller animal wouldn't have been so valuable.

Filled with the roasted pork, Billy Two stood up and stretched. He went over to the small pool by his campsite and dived in to wash himself. When he emerged out of the water, he went to turn the spit as he had regularly for the past few hours to make sure the pork was evenly cooked.

He was tired, very tired. It had been a long and strenuous hunt. He wished he had the luxury of sleep, but he knew he couldn't afford that. There was more work to do. He picked up the stone implements he'd been fashioning and went back to work on the pieces of green wood he'd found. They weren't birch, but they were young and supple and would more than suffice to make bows and arrows.

He assumed that the warrior followers of Hawk Spirit who had once lived on the island had used the same wood for their own weapons before they had gone to North America and had to use new forms of raw material. He enjoyed the idea and let his mind move into a vision of himself in the context of thousands of years of history.

There was so much to do in such a short time! He didn't let his hands rest idly simply because he was enjoying the daydream of history. He examined the other piece of timber he'd gathered. It was the trunk of a tree not unlike balsa, lightweight and extremely porous. He would move some of the coals from the fire to it soon, letting the hot stones burn into the log and hollow it out. He could fashion a sail from the boar's skin and from the other pelts he'd accumulated. It would be enough to take him to the holy island, the one that was said to belong to the devil because the true believers had been forced off it.

Billy Two struck the piece of wood he was working on too hard, and it was ruined.

I must control myself, he thought, and let my anger be directed to the enemies of Hawk Spirit. I am here to regain his temple and restore his priests. I am not here for myself.

He silently apologized to Hawk Spirit for his anger and went back to work. Fatigue blurred his sight, but he continued with his task. He wouldn't forget his goal. He would continue working for many more hours, caring for the fires, moving the coals, manufacturing his weapons, going on with the construction of his sailboat.

He would do his duty.

"WHY DIDN'T YOU TELL ME?" Gasteau yelled at Groting.

"It seemed unnecessary, Professor," the German answered defensively. "I told you there was a cruise ship in harbor. There are often thieves on board those things, ready to prey on the other passengers. They obviously thought they would try their hands at something in the town. It just seemed so clear—"

"Are you really that stupid, Groting? Do you really think that small-time con men are going to attempt to break into a house with three well-armed guards protecting it? Do you really think that any criminal so accomplished that he can eliminate such mercenaries would then turn around without taking anything? What an imbecile you are!"

"Professor—" Groting scowled slightly, hardening under the Frenchman's verbal assault "—I saw a situation, and I evaluated it with the help of the general."

"The general!" Gasteau was truly beside himself now. "The general is more stupid than you are. He wouldn't know a real crime from—Bah! Both of you are fools.

"And those Canadians, what the hell were they doing at dinner tonight?"

"They're harmless," Groting said stubbornly, maintaining his defensiveness. "You saw the woman, quite beautiful. The general enjoys her company, and he thinks the husband might invest in one of his modernization schemes."

"Like hell!" Gasteau wasn't even bothering to argue any more. Although his suspicions had been lulled about the Canadians, the unexpected development made him feel renewed doubt. "They're involved in this. I just know it."

"How can you say such a thing!" Groting got up and refilled both their cognac snifters. "They're nothing. They are hardly the types to take out our men. Besides, they were at the same reception I was. They couldn't have—''

Groting stopped himself short. Gasteau looked up at him, waiting for him to continue. ''No,'' the German finally spoke up again, ''there's no way—''

''What?'' Gasteau demanded.

''The man did leave for a bit, to drink wine with the ambassador. There's no way he could have gotten over here, done in the guards and returned. Besides, he was only wearing a tropical-weight tuxedo. I would have seen any weapons, even if he were trying to conceal them.''

''I don't want any more games with these 'newlyweds,''' Gasteau announced. ''This entire operation is much too important to take any chances. I think it's time for them to have an accident.''

''Too many of those going on as it is,'' Groting answered. ''Granted, no one asked any questions about that other couple—those older Americans—but...''

''There are no 'buts' anymore, Groting. We are almost ready for launch. My entire life is based on its success. So is the enormous investment our masters have made in this project. A few tourists can't be allowed to interfere or to endanger it in any way at all.

''All the best in European technology is out on that island. We have combed all of the best minds in our countries—those that haven't been fooled by the image of an Atlantic alliance with Washington.

''Once we make this launch, the balance of power will be inalterably changed. We will be the ones in charge of space. The Russians *and* the Americans will be the minor players in the arena of world politics. With a few controls, we will be able to eliminate them from the heavens.''

Gasteau was being swept up in his vision. His eyes were glazing over. The usual detached demeanor was gone, and in its place was the face of a fanatic.

''Think of it, Groting, our masters will be able to rule the world. We can forget the barbarities of the Communists, and the foolish democratic principles of the Americans, as well.

''With this missile, we'll be able to knock out every satellite that's been launched, and its armaments will be capable of shooting down every further attempt to replace Russian or American satellites.

''The European governments that have sold out to NATO or the Warsaw pact will fall in the face of our might, and a truly united front will come forth to show the world where civilization really sits and where learning truly rules.''

Groting was taken aback by the sudden outburst. ''Surely you're going too far, Gasteau. You don't think that the masters will do anything like that. They're after commercial success.''

''Oh, no.'' Gasteau stopped to sip some of his cognac. ''Power corrupts, Groting, and absolute power corrupts absolutely.

''You're correct, as far as you go. No one has said that the project will be used offensively. However, you will note that no one has stopped us from adding that potential to the missile.

''When the thing is in place in the heavens and our masters see just how much they could have by so easily removing any semblance of competition, you'll see how quickly their minds will change and how fast they will implement the next stage in all of this.

"After all, Groting, they didn't name the project after a pet bird. It isn't called the Canary or anything like that. It's the Peregrine Solution.

"Interesting choice of words, isn't it?"

"The peregrine hawk can be trained to kill on command. The other word, *solution* does lend a sense of finality to things, doesn't it?"

Groting wasn't going to go any further. He knew perfectly well what the owners of the Peregrine Solution had in mind. Gasteau was right, of course. They were after nothing less than world domination.

The satellites they were going to carry to orbit with this launch were, in reality, exactly what the American President wanted his own country to do with his Star Wars program. Unhindered by the extravagant waste of the American military and the gouging and profiteering of the United States military contractors, a conglomerate of German, French and Italian companies had brought together the best minds in their countries and let them loose to find a quicker and less expensive solution to the problems.

The Peregrine Solution was the answer. It had been an enormous enterprise, one that had taken a huge investment, even if it was much less than the Americans had supposed theirs would be. Unhindered by controls that United States laws imposed on research—respect for human life and civil liberties among them—the Peregrine Solution had moved more quickly than anyone could ever have imagined.

Finding a dupe like General Falanu had been one of the shortcuts to success. His willingness to rent Devil's Land to the conglomerate had assured them of the secrecy they needed, along with a geographical position that was perfect for their uses. The requirement of a launch site so close to the equator was easily met.

Still, Groting wondered just how much Gasteau did know about the undertaking.

He also wondered how the Frenchman had gotten involved. All the really legitimate minds in Europe had been involved with the Ariane or the Airbus. The underground conglomerate had been so successful in its recruitment of scientists and others such as technicians only because it was willing to overlook past transgressions and associations that had denied security clearances to the men and women involved.

Was Gasteau one of those with an unsavory sexual past? He was too young to have a Nazi background. Perhaps, though, like Groting, he was the son of someone who had been involved in that sadly unsuccessful attempt at German domination of the world. There had been, after all, many Frenchmen involved in the Vichy regime whose sons were as tainted by their fathers as Germans like Groting were.

Did Gasteau even understand the meaning of the word *Solution* in the Peregrine project?

Well, there was no need to wonder too much about it, Groting mused. He was Gasteau's overseer, the one who was politically and commercially responsible to their masters back in Europe.

Let Gasteau fume about a few guards who had probably been dealing in some black-market schemes of their own and who had been killed by some other petty criminals in revenge. They had been paying a fortune for these men, these mercenaries.

Groting shared one thought with Gasteau. "The men we have had to hire are less than what I would like."

The French scientist took to the change in conversation immediately. He obviously had been having the same thoughts. "What do you expect from such mongrels?" he asked. "Hired guns without passports, without countries of their own anymore.

"Rhodesians, Portuguese adventurers who no longer have an empire to bully, Americans with too much blood lust to tolerate life under their country's suffocating laws. This is hardly an army!"

Gasteau gestured dismissively. "It's a good thing that we don't have to count on them for anything of importance. The missile will be launched within the next three days. Our project isn't relying on strong-arm tactics for success. It is our corporate brains and the multinationals' technology that will decide the future of the world. We are past the days of the superman and the hero. In some ways, it's too bad. But the course of history has been charted by science. The individual has no force left, at least not any force other than what he can learn to do with computers and in the laboratory.

"We are the future, Groting, us and our masters. The time when history was being decided by soldiers in the field is past, gone forever. History from now on will be decided in the research offices of corporations. Individuals are done, finished as players in the game of world domination.''

Groting smiled. He knew it was true.

BILLY TWO FINALLY COLLAPSED from exhaustion. He barely had the strength to get to his bed. He sprawled out over the piles of soft leaves he'd gathered and looked up at the night sky once more before falling asleep.

''Come to my dreams, Hawk Spirit. Give me more strength for tomorrow. I have your work to do.''

But he wasn't awake for any answer. Billy Two fell into a deep sleep as soon as his eyelids closed.

9

Alex Nanos was back in the Dolphin bar the next afternoon. He'd taken to hanging out in the place, even given the risk to his liver posed by his friendship with Hank. It was obvious the other Greek was an unlimited source of invaluable information about the comings and goings in the harbor. If he had to sacrifice a vital organ for the sake of the mission, what the hell? Nanos reasoned. He'd risked other parts of his body for the SOBs before.

Alex had tried to get as much out of Hank as he could. He thought he'd been discreet with his inquiries, but when Hank sat down and began to talk, it was immediately obvious that he hadn't been careful enough.

"Look, my friend, what is it? Are you one of those mercenaries like the others, the ones that the foolish general hires? Huh? A good Greek like you sold out to these people?

"I worry about you like a brother. I don't like to see you tied up with these people." Hank's breath reeked of garlic and olive oil, the two ingredients present in everything he ate and forced on Alex.

Nanos was, even then, staring at a plateful of fresh fish that had been sautéed in the oil. He was picking his way through the luncheon, hoping that the motions of eating would buy him a few minutes to find the right answer.

"You try to avoid my question," Hank said, a hurt tone in his voice. "It only makes me more sure that you're in trouble."

"No, no, I'm not in any kind of trouble at all," Nanos tried to reassure his new friend.

"But you're so suspicious of everything that's coming and going in Matali."

"I just like to know what's going on, that's it," Alex insisted.

"If you would only ask honestly, maybe I could help you more."

Alex stared at the big man and realized that Hank was trying to hint at something. To find out for sure, though, caution was needed. "Hank, I don't want any problems. I don't want to get you in trouble."

"You wouldn't be doing that if you were on the other side," the restaurant owner answered slyly.

"What 'other' side could there be?"

"Anyone who wasn't with those hired guns over on Devil's Land; anyone who was opposed to the general and his trying to modernize this place."

Hank gave Alex a thoughtful look and leaned closer across the table. "You know how I got here? Huh? I was on a tramp freighter, a ship to no place in no hurry to get there. I was shipping out of San Diego—I told you I was born there—and I hit this hole.

"At first, I was like every other horny seaman: I just wanted to get on shore and get my rocks off. But I was thirty, worried about growing older, thinking about the future for the first time in my life—you know how it gets when you turn a decade older? That was me in those days.

"I think, friend, that something snapped when I got to shore on this place. I thought, this is where a man could grow old.

"The priests were in control. They still had their temple over on Devil's Land, but they would come over here all the time, and there were wonderful religious ceremonies. The beliefs of these people are... well, Alex, they're beautiful. They just want everyone to be happy and in tune with nature, and all of that.

"I stayed when the ship pulled up anchor. A tramp like that is used to losing some men in port, and they didn't waste any time looking for me.

"The only thing I knew about living on land was cooking. My father taught me that. I figured I could try and make a living at that. I started out with a little shack on one of the docks, and I saved my money. I even taught the locals a thing or two about growing some garlic.

"I was happy. I had been right. This was a place to grow old. Maybe even find a wife someday and have some kids. I shopped around, and I got me a local girl and she's got me some babies."

Hank cast a satisfied glance at Alex. "You didn't know that, about my kids. I don't like talking about them in a bar, and I had to get to know you before I could bring them up. The three of them got the local eyes, big dark-colored ones, but they got Greek features. And they're so loud they must have Greek vocal cords.'' Hank burst into his impressive laugh at that statement, as if to demonstrate his point.

''I want my kids to grow up nice, you know. I don't want to take them back to the States and have them doing drugs in junior high school or learning to talk dirty from television. I want them right here on this beautiful island with their mother's traditions and the religion.

''But that means I got to watch out for this general and what he's up to. I get nervous, Alex, when I see mercenaries walking the streets, and I get real upset when I know that the priests have been kicked off their holy island.

''Now, into all of this comes this countryman of mine, and he's asking all these questions about mercenaries. I wonder about that, and I wonder just what it is that he wants to do with them.

'' 'Does he want to join them?' I ask. Nah. That can't be. They don't recruit here in Matali. The priests are still powerful, and the locals aren't interested. Someone else is bringing in this bad bunch from other places.

''So that must mean that he wants to do something *to* them. Don't you think? Huh? This countryman of mine must be on the other side.''

The bar's owner seemed to delight in shrugging his shoulders and adopting an innocent expression to accompany his next words. ''Me? I don't even know what the sides are. I just know that my adopted country is in trouble and I want to do something. So maybe if this countryman of mine will come clean and ask some up-front questions, I can make life more easy for him, you know?

"Just so happens that I got these native men working for me, waiters, kitchen help. When I got the impression that there might be trouble coming and I realize that my life's savings are in my restaurant and my life's blood are my kids, I think that I should pay more attention to my own help, too. I think it might be worth my time to make sure the young guys I hire should know how to handle a boat, load and shoot a rifle, that kind of thing.

"Just insurance, you understand. Just in case this general person gets out of hand and the priests, they need some very *un*spiritual help.

"I got lots of ways to lend a hand to someone who might need it."

Hank looked around the restaurant. It was early, and there were no other paying customers.

"Hey, Makan!" Hank called, and the bartender looked over at his boss, who then yelled out something in the native tongue. The man smiled, reached under the bar and slammed a machine gun on the counter.

"Japanese," Hank announced, "their best. It's a Model 62. A 7.62 caliber with a belt carrying 250 rounds that it can get off in less than a minute. Not a pretty one, not one of those tiny things like an Uzi, but one that gets the job done, and well."

Alex was astonished. He looked at Hank with an open mouth.

"Now, friend, if you knew that I had a half dozen of those that I happened to have gotten from some friendly Japanese tourists, and if you knew that I had the same numbers of young men who know how to use them, what would you tell me I should be doing with all that, huh?

"Should I sit here and wait, just keep everything here to make sure that no one messes up my bar? Or do you have some better idea for me? Think maybe I should know about something that's going to happen on my island, and I should be prepared for it? Think maybe that the best defense is an offense, or something like that?

"I want some good talking from you, friend. I checked you out, by the way." Hank sat back and smiled, obviously pleased with what was going down. "You ain't from no ship. You flew in on Qantas. I got friends that work at the airport, and they remembered you when I asked. My brother-in-law also works at the airport, and he even looked up your reservation. You came in first class. You're a poor sailor looking for fishing work? Like hell you are.

"Talk, friend, talk a lot to me, and let's see what we're going to do with one another, huh?"

"WHAT HAVE YOU GOT, NATE?" Nile Barrabas was looking over his technician's shoulder. Beck was studying the radar screens in front of him and also a set of computer screens that were translating some of the data he'd picked up from his nearly constant surveillance of the activity coming from Devil's Land.

"Thank God for these computers with the new 80386 chips in them. They turn portables into amazing machines. I don't think I could have kept up with everything without them.''

"So what's the message?" Nile asked. He never understood what the man was saying once he began talking about his machines, and Nile didn't want to, either. He was just happy Nate was there to do his part of the job.

"What I have is a marked increase in activity. There's a lot of communication traffic going on via microwave between here and, I suspect, someplace in Europe. It's difficult to trace the destination of a microwave transmission; I'm only making a guess.

"There's also been a lot of traffic between Devil's Land and Matali. More boats have been going back and forth between the two in the past twelve hours than at any other time since we set up shop.''

"Did you get your answer from Jessup's people?" Nile asked.

"Yep, and that's positive, as well. The meteorological satellites that survey this part of the world are equipped with heat-sensing devices to monitor volcanic activity. Even though they can't 'see' through the supposed cloud cover of the island, they can pick up any deviation in its heat production. There's a report from one of them that there's a definite shift in thermal energy on the surface of Devil's Land. I think some *very* big engines are heating up, Nile, something maybe as big as a missile's rockets getting ready for a launch sometime in the very near future.

"Missiles don't just ignite or turn on, you see. They have to get going quite a while before actual blast-off.''

Nile stood up and swore under his breath. "We've got to go in there. The delivery from Jessup should be here, and soon."

"I think I've already picked it up on the radar screen, Nile. There's an unscheduled craft heading this way from Hawaii."

"I only hope that Jessup sent what we asked for."

"I still wish we were using choppers to get over there," Nate said. "We could use some much heavier artillery that way."

"Impossible," Nile answered. "We've seen too much about their defenses and the high-tech detection equipment they have. The Kevlar boat is the only thing I trust to get inside without their expecting us."

"You're right, as usual, Chief. It's just..."

"I know, Nate." Nile clapped the smaller man on the shoulder. "In any other place, at any other time, I'd just go in there shooting myself. This one calls for more complete planning. We're going to have to really depend on ourselves and our skills.

"Keep it up. I'm going to alert Claude and Liam about the plane's arrival."

"Way it's traveling, I'd give it another half hour before touchdown, Nile."

"I'll have them at the airstrip waiting for it," Nile answered.

LIAM O'TOOLE and Claude Hayes were on the tarmac when the aircraft approached. Nile was back with Nate, looking over some new data that had come in from Devil's Land.

"Shouldn't be long," Claude said. He was obviously bored. "You must have been getting some good time in on your poetry this trip out, O'Toole."

Liam was a closet poet, one who was determined to get his work into print and well distributed. His past in the Irish civil wars, his experiences in innumerable mercenary actions and his membership in the SOBs no more than equaled the importance of his writing.

"I'm missing a big writers' conference in Sonoma County" was all the Irishman could say in response. To Claude, his friend sounded as though he was saying he was missing the lay of his life. Sex was one of the few things in Hayes's existence whose importance even began to match Liam's love of his poetry.

"But you got plenty of time to write here. Hell, all the rest of them are the ones who have interesting things to do with their time over on the other island. At least there are women there!"

"You don't understand, Claude," Liam said. He'd tried to explain to the others so often that he couldn't hide the exasperation in his voice. "It's not just having free time. There has to be the inspiration. Here, there's nothing but sun and boredom. That's not what poetry comes from. It comes from the heat of experience, when the heart just has to sing out or burst from its pain and confinement."

"Sort of like a gospel tune, I suppose," Claude said. He did try to understand his buddy's addiction to verse, but it just didn't come easily to him.

"There's our baby!" Hayes said as a speck came into view on the horizon. "Least, I hope it is."

He picked up the binoculars and focused them on the airplane that seemed to be approaching. "What the hell..."

"Isn't that it?" Liam asked.

"I expected it to be either a military transport or something unmarked," Claude answered in an unsure voice.

"Well? What is it?" Liam insisted.

"O'Toole, my friend, it's polka-dot."

"Claude! For God's sake, stop with the stupid jokes."

Hayes didn't say a word. He just handed the binoculars to his friend. Liam took them and zeroed in on the plane that was now making an approach to the runway. The body of the craft was covered with large multicolored...polka dots. "Bejesus."

"Amen."

The plane's landing was erratic, to say the least. It was a Lear jet, the same plane that Geoff Bishop had used to deliver the SOBs to the island, but Bishop had put the thing down on the concrete as smoothly as a knife cutting butter. The pilot of the polka-dot plane wasn't up to any comparison. The Lear bounced hard on the first contact and then began a series of bumps and skips that left Liam and Claude convinced they might have a disaster on their hands.

They both breathed more easily when the Lear was able to halt just before it left the paved surface. The twin jet engines whined more loudly as they were revved up to power the plane over to where the two SOBs were waiting.

There was one final loud noise as the jets were shut down. The doors of the plane flew open and the stairs came out from their place inside the cabin.

"This thing couldn't have brought even the small list of stuff Nile sent to the Fixer," Claude said.

A single figure stood in the doorway and began to descend the stairway on wobbly feet. He was clearly very drunk and was carrying a bottle of Dewar's White Label in one hand. A pair of shapely blond women followed him out the door.

When he was halfway down the stairs, the man finally seemed to focus enough to realize he had a waiting party. "Who the hell are you?" he boomed out in a thick Scots accent.

"Who the hell are *you*?" Claude answered with an equal amount of gusto.

But Liam wasn't in the same frame of mind. "Don't you know?"

Claude turned to him and saw reverence on his pal's face. "No."

"It's Malcolm MacMalcolm," Liam said softly, "the greatest actor in Scotland, maybe in the world."

"Well, I think he made a wrong turn somewhere," Claude said to Liam.

"What the hell are you two doing on *my* island?" the Scots voice boomed once more. "Who the hell gave you permission to invade my privacy?"

"The actor!" Claude suddenly understood what was going on. "Hey, we rented this place from you. You're not supposed to be here."

"I own this island," the man replied. Trying to emphasize his proprietary interest, MacMalcolm took a grand step, not realizing he wasn't yet on the ground. He missed the next stair and went flying through the air. He managed to get his arms out in time to break his fall, but in the process he lost his grip on the bottle of Scotch whiskey, which shattered on contact with the concrete.

"Oh, damn!"

"There's more, honey," one of the blondes managed to say through her chewing gum. "I'll run up and get it for you."

"Sweet, nurturing love!" the man replied.

"What the hell are we going to do?" Claude voiced his disgust at the show. "This sure as hell explains that rocky landing. The pilot must be as drunk as the rest of them."

"Never trust a man who won't drink with you." The actor had overheard Claude and answered him even though he was still sprawled on the tarmac. "A man who won't drink with you won't die with you."

Claude was speechless at such ignorance. Liam was obviously more empathetic. He went over to Mac-Malcolm and gave him a hand, pulling him up to his feet and dusting off his soiled pants.

"It's a great honor to meet you. I saw your *Macbeth* at the Royal Shakespeare in London, and then I heard the recital of Scots ballads you gave at Carnegie Hall a couple years ago. I've never heard anyone giving a reading like that. You made them come alive. I thought I was in the Highlands, listening to the first shepherd as he was composing them, full of the wonder of his own creation."

"Carnegie Hall?" MacMalcolm wasn't too sure of his footing. "Was I there? Terrible place, you know. But one must pay the rent, and they do know how to cut a decent check in New York, what?"

"Here's your stuff, Mac." The blonde who'd gone to fetch a new bottle of Scotch was overtly proud that she'd been able to accomplish the task.

"We'll need glasses. We're on vacation, but one mustn't give up all the amenities simply because polite society isn't watching, must one? In the house!"

"Hey! You can't go in there!" Claude yelled at the man as he made his way toward the sprawling villa with theatrical strides and two blondes skipping on either side of him. "Liam, stop him."

O'Toole looked back at Claude; his face was a study in utter confusion. "But he's the greatest lover of poetry in the world!" And, as though that answered any possible problem, Liam started after the trio.

"God, I made it!" The pilot of the Lear was carefully walking down the stairway now, fervently holding on to the guardrails as he carefully took every step. "I can't believe I made it."

Claude was speechless.

Nate Beck came running out of the house. "It wasn't them?"

Claude pointed first to the inebriated pilot and then at the group that was going into the villa through the patio entrance.

"Well, that explains it. There's another blip on the radar headed this way. It must be Jessup's plane. But who are these jokers?"

"Nate, go on in the house and prepare yourself to meet our landlord."

"WELL, COUNTRYMAN?" Hank had been patiently waiting for Alex's return all afternoon.

"Something seems to have come up over at the private resort," Nanos said. "It took a while to get communications clear between everyone. But I have the high sign now.

"There's enough activity over on Devil's Land that we have to suspect they're going to move." Alex looked at the other Greek and hoped that he was doing the right thing by putting so much trust in him. He actually had little choice, even if he didn't want to.

The operation was going to call for much more manpower than one person could ever provide, and with Billy Two still among the missing, there wasn't much else Alex could do alone on Matali. His only remaining option was to break Lee and Geoff's cover. They presumably were taking care of other things and shouldn't be brought over for his part of the mission.

"We have to suspect that the fishing boats are cover for a top-secret, high-tech operation that some people none of us would like are carrying out. If my contact's speculations are correct—and they're seldom wrong—the boats are going to leave awfully soon to get into position for their part in the job.

"We have to stop them."

"And this will do something to remove the mercenaries from the general? We can get rid of that slob of a president?"

"What we have to do, Hank, is to get rid of the mercenaries, period."

Alex watched the other man as the message sank in. There wasn't much of an expression at first, but then a smile crept over Hank's face. "Then we will take care of the general himself."

"I think that's covered. We have our own job to do right now, though. Those boats can't leave harbor."

"If you say they mustn't, then they won't." Hank smiled. "I'll go and get my men."

GASTEAU WAS STANDING in the enormous control room built into the side of the peak of Devil's Land. The various screens were all sending out the messages he wanted to hear and believe.

They were within twenty-four hours of countdown.

"Give the order for the boats to proceed from Matali," he said to one of his officers. "The others should already be in position."

The man went off to make his call to the main island.

Gasteau walked through the cavelike room to the opening in the mountain where his brainchild was waiting in its cradle. It towered hundreds of feet above the floor of the plateau. Its sleek beauty was one of the most handsome things he'd ever seen.

The fools had tried to keep him from working on something like that. For years, the backwardness of the French scientific establishment had meant that scientists like himself were forced to play with primitive instruments while the Americans and the Russians had a monopoly on the truly advanced capabilities.

Then, even when France and other European countries had finally invested enough in their space and air programs, they wouldn't let a proven genius like Gasteau in on the planning and the implementation. All because of a few indiscretions in his past and their boring bourgeois attitudes toward morality.

Well, he would prove them all wrong. He had been the brains behind the Peregrine Solution. The money men might have come from the stock markets and from some of the great military families that had been discredited by the Algerian war, but he was the one who understood the Peregrine.

He had struggled most of his life to get to the head of a program such as this. He was going to succeed. Those fools at NASA and in the Ariane program were going to be humbled before him, and the idiots at the Kremlin were going to shake in their boots.

On that one missile there was enough superior technology to do them all in, once and for all.

It had to work, Gasteau summed up his stand mentally.

He dismissed the shadow of insecurity that crept through his thoughts. Everything depended on their getting just that one missile into orbit and in position to attack. If it didn't succeed, they were going to be discovered. Their means of shielding the existence of the Peregrine Solution worked only because no one was aware of it.

If Washington, Moscow, Paris and London knew what might be lurking on Devil's Land, then they could stop any second attempt.

The people who were bankrolling the Peregrine were there only because of its secrecy. Much of their support had been illegal. They had gotten the parts for the missile manufactured under false pretenses, telling any inspectors in their plants that the elements were for the Ariane or were subcontracted for some top-secret American project. If they were discovered, all of that would go by the wayside.

Gasteau's huge gamble would be for nothing. He would be ruined, uncovered and probably sent to prison.

He gritted his teeth. *The missile had to work!*

10

"But this is marvelous!" Even though Malcolm MacMalcolm was still consuming quantities of the Dewar's, he seemed to become suddenly much more sober. "It reminds me of *Flight over Zanzibar*. Did you see it?"

"I did, Mac," one of the blondes answered enthusiastically. "You were so macho in that flick that, ooh, I thought I'd faint from pleasure."

It was hard for even a fan as enthusiastic as Liam to imagine MacMalcolm's bloated body and alcohol-aged face in any kind of heroic role. But O'Toole tried to forget the current image of the actor and remember the man's former commanding presence. Before growing the bulge that pushed against his waistline now, and before the retreat of his hairline that left his balding head so obvious in the bright tropical sunlight, MacMalcolm had been one of the great male leads in theater and film. That was what Liam chose to focus on.

"Yes, yes, you would," MacMalcolm said, in a voice that was obviously meant to dismiss the woman's remark. He was much more interested in what Liam had just told him about the SOBs' presence on his retreat. Nile had decided that it would be best if the man understood just how much potential danger was involved. Maybe that would keep him out of their way and convince MacMalcolm that he should stay put.

"I don't see many movies," O'Toole admitted. "I like your live stage performances much better."

"Yes, of course, one like you would," Mac-Malcolm sighed, "but they don't pay for private resorts like this one, now do they?

"In any event, in *Flight over Zanzibar* I was a member of the British East African Army during the First World War. I had to defend Kenya against the Huns. It came down to my character's ability to fight by himself; the rest of the squadron was incapacitated. It was me...or the Germans. Only biplanes and that sort of thing, you understand, but it was the same idea as all of this, heroism and the love of war."

"I don't love war," Liam objected. "It's just sort of something that comes to me, fighting, that is."

"It's all the same, all the same indeed. The true masculine test, battle, struggle, all of it. I must study you and watch you as you go to combat, your manhood on the line, your existential frame of mind before the great test..."

"You do pretty good with *your* manhood," the other blonde said with a giggle. MacMalcolm shrugged out of her embrace.

"I don't really do anything like that," Liam said, embarrassed because it seemed that he couldn't come up with what the master craftsman wanted from him. "I have some poetry, though, about this, and if you'd like to read it..."

"The soldier-poet!" MacMalcolm jumped up. "There's a role in here for me! I know it." He turned his famous burning gaze on O'Toole and let it bore into the Irishman.

"I am not a fool." MacMalcolm paused dramatically, using all his stage training as he tried to talk directly to the SOB. "I know that my best days are gone. I still have command of the box office, though. I pick and choose my roles with care, and I know the next one must be my best." He threw a hand into the air and pointed toward the ceiling.

"Or else I'm going to have to sell this damned island and move into a condo in Santa Monica," he added in sudden despair. The image wasn't one that the actor liked, though Liam wasn't quite sure that the fate sounded as bad as all that.

"This could do it for me. Just think: A Rambo with soul. A *Platoon* that ends in victory! A *Soldier of Fortune* with poetry, for Christ's sake! It would have them screaming 'Oscar!'

"Of course, it would be novelized. Sequels are taken for granted. There's a good chance of a television spin-off in here somewhere. I could get a licensing deal for the dolls that would turn Wall Street's head. I can see a line of men's clothing! There are so many lucrative possibilities. . . ."

That was usually the point in any conversation when Liam tuned out. He was too mesmerized by the fact that his idol was standing in front of him to do that, however. And he had no defenses at all when the actor turned and pointed his finger directly at him.

"And it will all be based on your poetry. Go! Get it, man. I must read it. I must read the words of the warrior who has survived the battle to tell us what it is like to risk one's very *soul* for the sake of humanity. I want to hear the song in it all!"

Malcolm paused before his finale. "This is your big chance!"

Liam stood up. He was ignorant of the admiring glances he was getting from the two blond bombshells. He wore only his khaki shorts on the island, and his deeply tanned skin and his red hair was interesting them at least as much as the bank account and fame of MacMalcolm. But O'Toole was unaware, completely tuned out to that kind of vibration at that moment. He only knew one thing: a master of the stage was going to read his poetry and was even going to consider reading his words out loud.

"I only have a few things here," the Irishman said, speaking more quietly than usual, overcome by awe.

"But they're real, man! All the things I've been vetting in Hollywood were written by some fool sitting behind a desk who's never held a gun in his hands. You have been there. You're like the Greeks, the warriors whose songs are drenched with the reality of their battles. I must see you in action as well," the actor boomed.

"That's impossible, Mr. MacMalcolm. You have to understand, we never would have told you even as much as we have under normal circumstances. When the SOBs go into action, there's no way we can take on the responsibility of civilians."

"But I must become as real as you are. Don't you understand? The whole point is the veracity of the role. It must match the reality, or truthfulness, if you like, of the words in the script. Words that will come from your poetry!"

Liam blushed under his tan, but he couldn't soften. "It just can't be done."

"You are on my island!" The actor was trying to find some other string to pull to get his way.

"And we paid money for it. You weren't supposed to be here for another two weeks. Are you ready to give us back our rent?" Nile Barrabas said, calmly deflating the argument. The SOB leader had just walked in after getting a perfect fix on the man, and right away knew the key word in his vocabulary: money.

MacMalcolm seemed to calm down suddenly. Just as suddenly, the effect of the Scotch came over him again. He sat back on the couch between the two women and became ostentatiously glum. "The chance of a lifetime..." His words trailed off into silence.

He covered his face with one hand. The two blondes went into action, running their small palms over his shoulders and over his hair. "Want us to put on the grass skirts now, Mac?" one of them asked in an attempt to console the great actor.

"Hell, Nile," was all Liam could say.

Barrabas looked at his friend and knew better than to feed his mood right now with anything but an order. Whatever else he might be, MacMalcolm had been right when he'd pinpointed the essence of O'Toole: the man was a soldier, the real kind, the kind who understood the priorities of an assignment and the importance of carrying out orders.

"Forget this for now, Liam. We have more important things to worry about. We're going over to the island in twenty hours. Let's get ready."

No one paid any attention to MacMalcolm after that. They left the man alone with his companions.

BILLY TWO STOOD NAKED in front of the fire that burned by the sculpture of Hawk Spirit.

It was the midnight of the full moon, the time when the nameless old man had decreed the rites should be performed.

Billy Two held up the loincloth he'd made from the skin of the boar he'd hunted. He tied it around himself. It wasn't as well cured as he would have liked, but it was sufficient for its purpose now and would give him support he needed for his task.

The priest nodded knowledgeably and then continued his chanting. As he began to sing the songs for a warrior's preparation for battle, the young girls approached the nearly naked Osage with great deference and respect.

In their hands were the paints. The traditions decreed that no one should go to his enemy unadorned. The girls dipped their slender fingers into the bowls and then lifted them up to touch Billy Two's face with careful, delicate strokes.

He closed his eyes and imagined himself in the war camp of the Osage centuries ago. He was going through the same ritual his ancestors had taken part in, and it was close to the way they had done it, he was sure. He told himself to remember every detail of the moment, to treasure the memory of a man being made ready to defend his people.

Some of the hands moved down over his unclothed chest, leaving their traces there. Others moved over his thighs, leaving him with a tingling feeling unlike any he'd ever had before. He was feeling so much more than he'd ever experienced.

Then, just as the priest's chants ended, the girls stood back, their heads bowed, their job done.

Billy Two looked down at himself and saw the markings, designs more handsome than any he'd ever seen before.

The priest held up a brightly polished piece of bronze so Billy Two could see his face. There were sharply edged red chevrons streaking down the side of his skull. "Those give you the eyes of the hawk, to see your prey."

Then the priest stood back and pointed to his chest. There were more red depictions there that looked like lightning bolts painted on his pectorals. "Those are the Hawk's talons, coming out of your soul to grasp your enemy in your deadly grip."

On Billy Two's legs were blue and deep-green stripes that wrapped around his thighs and his naked flanks. "Those are the bands of armor the Hawk gives you. You need no more when you do his bidding. The arms of mere mortals will not harm you if you are under his all-seeing protection."

Billy Two picked up a belt, which was a much thicker and heavier piece of boar's pelt than the one that secured his loincloth. From it hung the boar's tusks and the sharpened ribs Billy Two had taken from its body.

From some of the bones he'd shaped handles, and for others he had only made holes at their thickest part so they could be hung from the belt, which was a kind of primitive moving arsenal.

"The Hawk will protect you, and you will defend the Hawk's people," the priest intoned, waving a blessing over the weapons.

Billy Two next picked up the bow he'd made himself, then the container of arrows he'd tipped with sharp pieces of stone he'd found in his retreat. He hung the quiver across his chest. He looked down at the visible part of each of the arrows jutting from the top of the container.

He had made them with the feathers of the birds of Matali. But none of them, to his chagrin, had come from a hawk. The falcon had ceased to exist on the island, his spiritual home. There were only songbirds and sea gulls on Matali now. Their feathers should do the job, and Billy Two had tested his arrows to make sure their progress was straight and to the target, but he desperately wanted to have hawks' feathers in his arrows.

He lifted one hand and felt the one feather that hung from his earlobe. At least that was there, a part of him, as he was getting ready to go into battle for his god. Hawk Spirit was with him.

He smiled suddenly and realized that the god's totem, which was made an actual part of his body by the piercing, was something even more real than feathers on an arrow would be.

The priest gave a new signal, and he began to lead Billy Two and the rest of the participants in the ritual down from the hill. They were going to the ocean, to the place where Billy Two's craft was waiting.

The boat was much more primitive than he would have liked. It wasn't even so smoothly constructed as the outriggers the native fishermen used, but he had made it with his own hands, the major requirement the priest had demanded.

When they got to the water's edge, Billy Two looked at the hollowed-out log and the makeshift sail that rose from it. He only had to go a few miles, and he was sure it would be more than adequate.

The priest had told him how to navigate his way to Devil's Land by the moon and the stars. It had seemed strange to Billy Two when the old man had given him those directions. Inside, somehow, he'd known that they were unnecessary. He never doubted his ability to find the god's real temple. His soul would have guided him.

His soul might not have known about the secret entrance to the temple, though, and that was information that Billy Two had gratefully accepted from the old man. The other two approaches to the island would be heavily guarded. It was one of the signs of the dim-wittedness of the uninitiated that they had never found the privileged entrance to the god's place.

Billy Two took the craft, and with the congregation singing once again, he moved it to the water. The boat wasn't even fully rigged, but the priest had suggested a means of sailing it that was not unlike windsurfing to Billy Two's mind, and he'd mastered the sport years ago.

He stood in the hollow of the log now, holding the controls to the sails and listening to the voices of the people whose future he held in his hand. He looked up to see a flock of sea gulls crying in the sky. Damned scavengers! They were like the intruders who defiled the temple, noisy, dishonorable beasts who wrongfully took the place of Hawk Spirit.

The wind took hold of the sail, and the boat was propelled out onto the Pacific. The voices of the people increased in tempo and intensity as Billy Two began his journey. Their fate was crossed with his own, and they knew it.

Billy Two saw the characteristic fin of a shark break the surface of the water. The primitive hunter of the sea thought it might have an easy catch for its dinner. Billy Two smiled at the symbol of danger.

He was under the care of Hawk Spirit. He wouldn't be harmed because he was the one who was going to do harm.

"YOU'RE SURE about these men?" Alex asked Hank once more.

"Friend, these aren't just any locals. You think I hire just anyone? These are my wife's nephews and cousins. The bond of the family on Matali is one of the strongest these people understand. I'm one of them now, after all these years. They understand that, and they'll stay with me.

"Besides, you have to understand that, no matter how easygoing the people are here, they loathe the general. If the priests had only told them to rise up, they probably would have done it with their bare hands. They've only waited because the priests have said they were waiting for some sign. We're giving them the chance to act *now*, and they're happy for it.''

Nanos didn't need any more encouragement. There were six native young men, each one holding one of the Japanese Model 62s. They all handled their machine guns with the assurance that only real training can give to a fighting man. The lethal weapons were cradled lovingly in their arms. They were ready, just the way Hank had said they would be.

''Let's do it,'' Nanos said. The word had come down to stop the fishing boats from leaving port, and the order had come none too soon.

Alex and Hank had watched as some other order had spread from trawler to trawler in the harbor. There was some last-minute racing for supplies from the mainland. It was obvious the boats were going to leave, and soon.

The native men had gathered together some of the outrigger canoes so common in this part of the South Pacific. Their cover was perfect. What could be more natural than some of the Matalians going out to fish?

The signal was given, and the men all took their places. There were four teams of two each, including Alex and Hank, who paired up with different younger men. The only one whom Nanos had known before was Makan, and it had been agreed they would team up.

Makan was no more than twenty years old. He wore the wraparound that was the common native dress, and nothing else. He directed Alex to lie on the bottom of the outrigger. The Greek would be too noticeable if anyone took the care to examine the inhabitants of the boat.

The outrigger took off from the beach that lined the harbor of Matali. Points of departure for the rest of the teams were spread out over the sand, another protection against anyone noticing anything strange about their joint launching.

"We're getting close," Makan said in the streetwise English that he'd learned from Hank. "The rest of the guys are moving in on them.

"No time to lose. There are a couple of the trawlers starting up their engines. We're going to head to the entrance of the harbor and be able to cut them off. Yahoo! Cowboy, we're going to eat 'em alive."

Nanos stayed on the floor of the large sail-rigged canoe and began to sweat. Like any other soldier, he hated that kind of hidden waiting. He would much rather be sitting up, his machine gun already pointed and ready to fire. Listening to Makan was as unsatisfying as trying to follow a World Series baseball game on radio.

But men had done that for decades, hadn't they? Alex closed his eyes tightly and tried to recreate the images that Makan was reporting to him.

"My buddy Kan is there! He closed them off. He's slacking on his sails, slowing his outrigger down! He's turning! There's his firepower, Samsula! He's aiming! *Fire!*"

The sound of automatic rounds filled the air. Alex jumped up at the signal and rested his own Model 62 on the outrigger's hull. He swept the area, and in his sights caught a pair of men scrambling around the foredeck of one of the fishing boats.

He squeezed the trigger and felt the recoil of the Model 62 pound into his armpit as its sweet song of metal exploding into the air filled his ears. The line of bullets danced a quick chorus line across the wooden planking of the trawler's deck, interrupted only when the rounds found their mark.

Then it was the hired hands' turn to dance.

The rapid fire of the Model 62s lifted up the once-living torsos and made them jump like marionettes on strings. Their arms waved obscenely in the air and their legs kicked incoherently. Then the lifeless bodies collapsed onto the deck in a flow of blood.

All over the harbor, the sound of automatic fire reverberated. The Matalians were ready, anxious to finally have the chance to act in their struggle against the general and the fools he'd imported to destroy their way of life. Their honor had been marred by the sale of their birthright, and they reveled in the chance to reclaim it.

The mercenaries on the boat were totally surprised by the uprising. None of them was really ready for the attack from the native canoes they had assumed were so innocent and so harmless.

A few managed to survive long enough to get into the cabins and grab their own weapons to try to repulse the onslaught.

But nothing fuels battle lust like righteousness, and the men of Matali were full of it. They found a fierce urge to do the right thing at any cost and were filled with emotions they never knew existed.

War cries sounded throughout the air. Alex saw Kan fall, his chest ripped open by rapid fire from one of the enemy vessels.

Nanos followed the line of bullets back to a fishing vessel that was in the middle of the pack. Two uniformed men were standing by the cabin, their rifles pouring torrents of hot metal into the outriggers.

Alex sighted down his Model 62 and triggered a burst. The first target didn't even have a chance to turn around and see who had caused his death. The line of Alex's fire tore through his neck, severing his skull from his body. He slumped to the deck.

His compatriot at least had his moment of recognition. He'd turned and begun to lift his own M-16 up to his shoulder, ready to return the assault. But Nanos was ready, was actually waiting. In his sights he saw the point where the line of eyebrows met just above the nose. He pulled the Japanese machine gun's trigger and watched the doomed man's face explode into an orgy of blood. The Greek looked away grimly and swept the harbor with his eyes to evaluate the current situation.

The fishing trawlers were now all disabled. Those whose engines were still running were beginning to move across the harbor in haphazard and undirected paths. Two of them collided, and both of them began to sink from the damage they'd inflicted on each other.

The Matali men yelled louder when their victory was obvious, drunk with the heady elation of successfully carrying off the surprise attack.

Alex sat down in the outrigger and gave Makan a thumbs-up, then began to prepare another belt of ammunition for the Model 62, just in case there was some lingering danger left in the cabins of the fishing trawlers.

He looked up at Makan's smiling face while he worked. There was only the flush of victory there now, but Nanos knew there'd be something else later, something more.

Alex had seen Kan die. The realization and acceptance of a man's death was something that he, a professional soldier, was used to, but Makan wasn't. So far he was only registering the wonder of victory. Sometime soon he'd have to see the price they had paid to achieve it.

Nanos made a promise to himself that when the time came he'd be there for the younger man. There were times you just had to do that for someone you fought with.

APPARENTLY LEE HATTON WAS ENJOYING the attention she was getting at Herr Groting's dinner table.

She smiled endlessly at the other guests—all of them male. The general was particularly receptive to her charms once again as she seemed to banter about meaningless topics that he would want to hear a "lady" discuss.

Lee was carrying on about the possibilities of incorporating some of the native Matali designs she'd seen on the streets and in the marketplace into the latest fads in interior decoration back in Montreal. She was sure, she told the assembled group, that the chic Quebecois would "adore" the authenticity of the forms and colors in the images that the Matalians seemed to specialize in.

Geoff Bishop sat there and had to fight to retain his own role as the brash young businessman. He was shocked that Lee could so easily fall into the facade of empty-headed gentility.

So far as Geoff was concerned, Lee was the hard-assed M.D., the doctor who was ready, willing and able to cut open a wound and perform an emergency operation without anesthetic. He'd watched her pull bullets out of men's chests, shrapnel out of children's bellies and bomb fragments from women's legs without blinking an eye.

She was the one who'd insisted that she be treated as a full member of the SOBs, and who had, from the start, demanded that she be put through the same grueling training as the men. There would be no special consideration given for her father's daughter, she'd insisted.

Nile Barrabas and the other SOBs had granted her that wish and had pushed her to the limits of human physical tolerance in their time together.

They'd all gotten used to seeing her in the field. Only Geoff was really privy to much of her private life. Still, he'd never seen anything about her or her personality that had hinted at the well-bred image she was projecting now.

Was it the remnants of her education at the private girls' school and the undergraduate college she'd attended? Someone had certainly taught her the proper way to pour tea; not one of the ultrasophisticated men who sat at Groting's was finding fault with her technique, that was for sure.

Geoff was watching her carefully when he heard the first shots from the harbor. The sound was faint, almost indistinct to the untutored ear, but his ear was anything but unschooled. He could identify the sounds of automatic rifle fire as quickly and as definitely as a mother would know a baby's cry.

A broad smile crept across his mouth. Lee looked up at him and caught the expression. She answered with her own grin, then slammed the teapot down on the table.

"The party's over, gentlemen."

The other men, even the general, didn't understand what was going on, and for a fatal split second they didn't respond to the lady's uncharacteristic outburst.

That was all the time Lee needed to reach down under the table and retrieve her large handbag. It had just been a topic of conversation, one of her displays of the commercial possibilities of Matalian handicrafts. The purse was large, with many compartments woven into its straw structure. It was also sturdy. In fact, it was sturdy enough that it had concealed a pair of Colt .45 autoloading pistols.

Lee tossed one of the weapons across the table to Geoff. Bishop's face broke into a huge smile, and he yelled out a remark that only confused the other men more, "That's my girl! It's about time!"

Then they began their attack. First they took out the four guards who were standing with Karlsrupa automatic rifles at the doorway. The mercenaries simply collapsed to the floor as the rapid-fire pistol rounds ripped through them.

Then the pistols were turned on the general and Herr Groting, as well as their aides, who were still all stunned into inaction at their places in the table.

The room reeked of cordite from the expenditure of the bullets, and the cloying odor of blood was beginning to make its way from the corpses that were slumped on the floor around the walls of the dining area.

The quick movements of the two trained SOBs had actually been enough to petrify the other dinner guests, but the image of Lee Hatton they were looking at now was just as compelling.

The once delicate and not-too-smart Mrs. La-Liberté was now standing up with her legs spread wide in the practiced stance of a marksman, her knees bent, her hips thrown back. Holding the deadly Colt in both hands, she swept it over the assemblage, daring any one of them to move.

"The general's got something in a shoulder holster, Geoff. I saw the bulge. Better check the rest of them, too." Lee then gave the company her full attention. "All right, all of you, hands up. Reach for the ceiling *right now*. I warn you, if you so much as hesitate, I'll blow your brains out."

The men somehow got the order transmitted from their minds to their limbs, and extended their arms upward.

"Good boys. Now, slowly, stand up and make your way over to the far wall. The first one who lets down his hands is going to sleep for a long, long time."

The men slowly followed the woman's bidding. The minute when they were all up against the wall, Geoff moved quickly to spread their legs with sharp kicks at their calves. He used his free hand to slam their heads against the wood paneling, though never losing his grip on his own Colt.

The sounds of gunfire from the harbor were increasing in frequency.

"You're fools!" the general spat out. "Can't you hear my army? You're going to end up in front of a firing squad."

"You know, General," Geoff said as he removed the pistol from the general's shoulder holster, "I don't think you got that quite right."

Geoff ignored the rest of the man's complaints and moved along the line of captives, making sure none of them were armed. When he was done, he stood back and threw a wink at Lee. "So good to see you in character again," he said with a sigh. "I thought I was going to spend the rest of my life with a perpetual debutante."

"Aren't you? Do you think I'm not quite feminine enough, Geoff?" Lee smirked back at him.

Her voice changed when it was time to address the prisoners once again. "All right, now, *slowly* move your arms down and put them behind yourselves."

"You're making a grotesque mistake," Groting said.

"No, we're not, Groting. We know exactly what we're doing and just what you think you're doing, as well. Don't make the mistake of thinking that this is a simple theft that's going on. We couldn't care less about your money. We're here to stop your little plan for a space outfit. Seems that there are some people who don't like to have competition in that particular area."

When he heard Lee speak, Groting found something inside himself, and he displayed it now. If it wasn't really courage, it was at least something to do with backbone, more than the rest of them had displayed. His voice was thick with venom. "You're going to pay dearly for this outrage. Do you think that your Wild West show is sufficient to stop our enterprise? We're going to rule the world, and you think you can come in here and—"

"And you think we're alone, do you?" Lee interrupted him. "You should realize better than that, Herr Groting."

The German's shoulders slumped for a moment but then came up again to take on that proud posture of his. "You will not succeed. We will be victorious."

Just then, there was a louder and more pressing round of automatic fire from the harbor. Geoff moved over to one of the sets of windows and looked out. "Sorry, General," he reported, "it looks like the good guys are winning this round."

11

The Kevlar boat rushed across the Pacific, racing toward its destination.

Nile Barrabas, Claude Hayes and Liam O'Toole were once more in their night cammy, even though dawn was about to break. There was enough time before sunrise to warrant it, and in any event, there would still be some benefit to the darkness of the grease that covered them. One of the main purposes of camouflage isn't to actually obscure a person, but to blunt the lines of his body, making it more difficult for a marksman to get an accurate fix.

That's why tree and bush branches are so often used in the battlefield. It isn't just that a man's appearance can be erased—though it sometimes can be when he's at a great distance from his foe—but that the enemy is also left without a clear and identifiable outline of the man's body, and especially of his ultimately vulnerable head. The blurred image makes it much more difficult for accurate shooting, a difficulty that has meant the difference between life or death for many soldiers in the field.

The dark cammy grease would keep any of the defenders on Devil's Land from making the SOBs out too clearly, and when the men were in the many shadows thrown by the crevices and gullies of the volcanic rock, their opponents would have a much harder time getting a fix on them.

Nate was at the controls of the powerful cigar boat once more. He was itching to be in on the attack, but his role was the care of the hardware. He understood that. The support personnel of any operation had a vital part to play.

The trio of SOBs who'd take out the missile site were standing on the extreme foredeck. The wind whipped through their hair and bit their skin.

The minutes before battle. Nile Barrabas had been there before, often. The responsibility of leading troops into combat was something he'd never taken lightly. No leader of men could. It was his duty to make sure the plan was as airtight as it could be. He was the one who had to decide which of the men was at point—in the most vulnerable up-front position— and who were the ones for the hold-back slots, places from which superior marksmanship might make the difference between victory and defeat.

The peaks of Devil's Land came into Nile's view. The gray of early dawn blunted the sharpness of his vision, just as the camouflage would work on an enemy's ability to see him. Still, the target was there, without doubt, its ominous presence rising up out of the ocean and soaring toward the heavens.

It was like a Gothic cathedral, he realized. The medieval architects had designed those lofty structures in such a way that a human's sight was forced upward, into the skies. Just so, Nile, looking at the towering mountain, found his own gaze lifted toward that place that some men would have called heaven.

He thought about Billy Two at that moment. He didn't know why. The disappearance of the Osage was a personal loss to him, as it was to all the other SOBs. He simply couldn't believe that Billy Two had left them stranded. It was just as impossible to think that the proud Osage had ever been caught by one of their enemies.

Nile recognized that the stresses they had all been under the past few years had been extreme. They were constantly called on to operate at their peak in the most fearsome and difficult situations any man could ever imagine. Perhaps it wasn't so strange that one of them would break.

He swore at himself for not having recognized more clearly the psychological danger that Billy Two had been faced with. If he had, he could have ordered the Osage to stay in the States, away from their strangely dangerous assignment. Or, at the very least, he could have assigned him to tasks such as piloting the speed-boat. It was unquestionably an important part of the operation, but one that wouldn't have put Billy Two in the field, facing armed opponents and under pressure to come up with the undefinable ability to keep his mind together in one piece.

When they got back, and if Billy Two was with them—the thought burned in Nile's mind—he'd demand a full workup by Lee Hatton. He'd have her, as the medical doctor on the squad, get to the bottom of the strangeness that the Osage was showing and find a treatment.

If there was one.

Nile forced himself back to the present, evading just the kind of distraction that the leader of an assault team couldn't have in his mind with the battle drawing near. Whatever was to become of Billy Two would be in the future, after the attack on Devil's Land. Right then, compassion for a friend was something a leader couldn't afford.

Nate Beck piloted the boat up to the beach they'd used before. The nose of the craft touched the black sand, and the three SOBs who were going to be making the trip up the steep embankment jumped off the boat onto land. This time they had to pull the cigar boat in toward the shore. The cargo they were carrying was too heavy to simply pass over the long foresection of the speedboat.

"Damn it!" Claude Hayes swore as he and Liam struggled to get the big weapon out onto firm ground. "This thing's supposed to be on a jeep or some other mechanical horse."

"It works just as well on a tripod," Nile answered. "If you think it's too heavy to carry up to the top, I'll do it myself."

Claude only snorted. He wasn't about to let anyone claim that he had shirked a little bit of hard work. His pride now demanded that he carry the MK-40 himself. "You get the stand for this sucker," he said to Liam. Then Claude shot a defiant grin at Nile. "Come on, boss. I'm ready to do my mule duty."

Liam and Nile each had their own heavy loads to carry. They had full-size M-16s. The automatic rifles were equipped with armor-piercing rounds specially made to break through some of the thickest defenses yet devised. They weren't playing games, and they weren't looking for ease of handling alone. They had wanted real firepower, and they had it.

The men made their way up the trail they'd found by the waterfall during their first surveillance. Claude had to use his considerable muscle power to drag the heavy MK-40 on his back. Sweat poured down over his face, running into his eyes and making him stop occasionally to let Liam wipe it out of the way so he could see where his next foothold was.

They made the top after a half-hour climb. Liam led the way, going over the edge of the slope first to make sure they weren't stumbled on by one of the guards. He crawled on his stomach once he'd reached the flat plateau, checking out a wide area before going back to signal the other two men.

He was all ready to send his message when two men moved toward him, just barely walking into his vision in time. If they had appeared even a few seconds later, he might not have spotted them, and they could have gotten a take on Nile and Claude as they appeared from their protective spot underneath the rim of the plateau.

Liam quietly removed the straps of the boxes he'd been carrying up from the beach and left them and the rounds of ammunition they contained on the ground. He knew he had to maintain total silence. He used his elbows and his knees to propel himself over the ground, ignoring the way the sharp rocks of the surface bit into his stomach and tore through the fabric of his shirt and pants.

The discomfort was nothing, not while he had those other two men in view. They had to be eliminated before he could get the other guys up here and into action.

The pair of uniformed men were carrying Karlsrupas like the guards they'd found on their previous visit. They were being more vigilant about their duties, though. Even if the ones in charge had bought the setup of the men having broken orders and gone swimming, security had been tightened.

Liam wasn't going to have the advantage of utter surprise, and he was also going to have to move on both men at once.

They were speaking to each other softly; that was already an indication that they were better soldiers than their careless predecessors, who had been so nonchalant in their conversation. These two men were scanning the area carefully as Liam stuck close to the ground.

He reached down and carefully took the knife he carried out of its sheath. He put it between his teeth and bit down to get a good hold on it, forcing himself not to gag at the taste of the machine oil he'd used to clean and sharpen the blade with. The flavor of the petroleum-based material was almost nauseating.

But a stomachache was the least of his troubles, and he knew it.

His big hero MacMalcolm should see him now, he thought. There was the obnoxious taste in his mouth, and from his body there was a flow of sour-tasting sweat, the kind of perspiration that fear and extreme tension produce. MacMalcolm would probably like to think in terms of masculine odors and that kind of foolishness. Liam was only aware of the fear.

It wasn't the sort of fear most people experienced, the emotion that threatened to incapacitate a man and leave him unable to act. The stink that came from Liam now and the sensation that was producing it were both welcome companions for any soldier worth the name. They were the stuff that kept a soldier alive, that made him alert, conscious of everything around him because he knew that missing the slightest thing could mean his own death. It was the fear that came from a primeval sense of self-preservation.

It was the fear that these two guards didn't know. And Liam knew that was what was going to kill them.

Timing was crucial at this point. He had two enemies who were trying to protect themselves. He had to follow their slow and careful movements and detect the pattern in them. He thought he saw it and knew he would have to chance it. The only option was to let them go on, and since the SOBs didn't know the routine of the guards well enough, that could mean that they'd have two armed foes too close for comfort just when they were going to be most vulnerable themselves.

The men were visually searching the area around them in a synchrony that was probably unconscious. Just as the one on the right would look to his right, the other one would turn to his left.

They were moving closer to Liam. The Irishman knew that they were making a major mistake, one that many fighting men made and few lived to regret. They were scanning the area around themselves at their own shoulder level. They would see Nile and Claude if the two men climbed out onto the plateau, but they weren't looking underneath them, and that was where Liam was.

His black-greased body and his black clothes also let him blend into the ebony rock of the island. His red hair was carefully concealed by a watch cap.

They moved even closer. Liam could make out the laces on their boots as they passed by him, not seeing his form. He'd even held his breath as long as he could, not even wanting the movements of his chest's expansion and contraction to alert them to his presence.

Then they were past him. He moved stealthily. He prayed that the leather in his own footwear wouldn't squeak as he stood up. Taking the knife from his mouth, he held it in his hand. He watched carefully, timing the movements of the two guards' heads.

At the precise moment when the one who was now on his own left turned to scan off in that direction, Liam leaped forward with all his strength.

The knife ripped downward, beginning at the rear of the man's neck, tearing through his back, exposing his spinal cord. When the blade had traveled far enough to be close to the vital organs, Liam tore it sideways, puncturing the lung and then piercing the heart.

The other man couldn't even react before Liam had the knife out of its first target. Now Liam took the blade and shoved it into the side of the new mark's abdomen. Liam knew that a simple puncture wouldn't do the job. There had to be something more. He twisted the blade quickly so that it was perpendicular, then ripped upward, cutting through liver and spleen.

Blood poured out of the two bodies as they collapsed, shocked into silence for their last living seconds.

Only after he'd lifted up their heads and sliced their necks for coups de grace that insured their departures did Liam signal his comrades to come over the top.

Claude made it over the edge and sprawled on the ground. Nile moved quickly to take the MK-40 off him while Liam set up the tripod. When the large weapon was finally removed, the big black man got up on his knees and began to massage himself.

There was no time for the niceties of conversation. Nile and Claude saw the two corpses and their slow streams of blood and understood what had caused the delay. They didn't have time to say anything to Liam right now. He didn't expect it; he didn't need their approval. Let Malcolm MacMalcolm talk about the glories of war and battle; all Liam wanted right then was to forget the sensation of the blade cutting through human flesh.

No matter how often he did it, no matter how convinced he was of the cause that made him commit those acts, he knew once again what he had always, in fact, known. He hated death with a passion that was only matched by his love of life.

Nile and Claude ignored all of it and, instead, went to work surveying the scene in front of them. The activity around the enormous missile that sat in the middle of the clearing was proof enough that the men had little opportunity to do anything but act and act immediately.

The MK-40 was ready. Liam nodded to Nile. Claude was up on his feet and had taken the M-16 that Liam had brought to the summit. He, too, nodded to the leader. The attack was set.

Liam started the deadly fire of the MK-40.

One of the newest weapons in the American arsenal, the machine was designed to clear a field of fire. That meant more than a little shoving and pushing aside of an enemy. It meant that the thing was there to remove *all* opposition in its way.

Liam checked the belt of coffee-can-size ammunition once more. The 40 mm rounds were ready. He began.

The MK-40 spit out its sure death onto the plains of Devil's Land. The first one of the canisters landed near the base of the missile. It exploded with a fearsome roar. The thing was essentially a large grenade. It shot a huge amount of shrapnel into the air, cutting down anyone and anything within dozens of feet of its target.

There had been at least twenty-five men milling around the foot of the missile launch. They had been wearing protective gear of some kind. Nile watched as the MK-40 tore through their bodies, and then he realized that the bits of hot metal from the canisters were doing something just as lethal when they tore open the suits.

The missile's fuel must have been poisonous. There were men who were so far away from the explosion that they shouldn't have received a fatal wound from it, but they were clutching their throats, stumbling with dying steps, trying vainly to escape the fumes that were suffocating them.

Those men were hundreds of yards away from the SOBs' point of attack. Nile didn't have a chance to observe them any longer, because Liam was using the weapon in just the way it was supposed to be used.

He was sending off a single round every few seconds, carefully calibrating his aim with each one so that the canisters were each exploding in a slightly more shallow field of fire. The ignition of the grenades was full of deadly effect. The bodies of the scientists and the technicians who were closest to the missile went down first, but surprise and deadly accuracy left the armed guards who were nearer the SOBs unprepared and unable to defend themselves.

In a matter of a few minutes, Nile was able to see the floor of the plateau littered with the dead corpses of the enemy. There hadn't been time for heroics because there hadn't been time for any kind of response at all. There had only been time for the MK-40 to do its job.

Nile gave the signal. The MK-40 was abandoned. Liam picked up one of the Karlsrupas the guards had dropped, and the three of them began their race across the plateau, heading for the headquarters of the missile site.

Even if they hadn't done their surveillance, they would have spotted it easily from the reactions of the few armed guards and scientists who had survived the MK-40 attack. Those men had all raced for the enclosure at the edge of the missile site.

Now came the human dimension of the assault. Technology had prepared the way. Soldiers had to follow up.

BILLY TWO HAD NEVER QUESTIONED his ability to make it to Devil's Land, but as he approached the black rock island, he still felt a wave of excitement move through his body.

The soaring rocks were the home of his god; it was the site of the defiled temple; it was the place where Hawk Spirit had sent him to meet his fate.

History coursed through his veins; destiny crowded his sense of himself. He was acting for a power far greater than his ego or his personality.

He looked up into the heavens and silently prayed to his god that he would be able to do the task ahead of him. The priest had said that he would discover his own worth in the coming confrontation. If he was inadequate, he would die.

The small craft he'd constructed finally came to the shore of the island. There, on the east side, he found the sacred way that the priest had promised him would be there.

Billy Two jumped off the craft and caught a precarious handhold. He had to struggle to get his feet into the tiny clefts in the rock. That was the "ladder" the old man had told him about. Only by carefully studying the side of the mountain could Billy Two find the small indentations in the stone that would allow him to climb up the sheer side of the island.

No one would be guarding the unknown approach to the plateau. No one could ever have imagined that there was any possibility that a mere mortal could ascend that slope.

Slowly, all his muscles screaming at the agony they were suffering as they were called upon to lift him farther and farther up the rock, Billy Two made his way.

He wondered at the ancient people who had constructed the devious method of ascent. If he, with his constant training and top physical condition, found progress difficult, what must the men have been like who not only climbed but also carried the tools to mark each successive indentation in the hard stone?

It was the blackness that made it difficult to find each of the small steps in the rock. The natural shadows hid the constructions, making the holds disappear into the ebony facade.

He never thought about giving up. Even if he wanted to, there was a certain point of no return in the enterprise. Once Billy Two was more than halfway up the mountain, he knew that going down would be at least as straining as continuing upward.

Below him, the Pacific Ocean surf crashed against Devil's Land. He could see that his boat had been battered against the rock so hard that it was already beginning to disintegrate under the horrible use it was taking.

Billy Two rested only briefly and smiled to himself when he realized that there was only the possibility of victory now. There was no way to return to Matali. There was no boat to take him across the waters to the main island. Only the struggle to succeed and the hope of righteous victory was ahead of him.

He kept on going.

Occasionally one of his feet would lose its perch, and he would have to hang on with his fingertips as they gripped the small indentations. Once both feet slipped, and he nearly went toppling backward into the waiting arms of the ocean.

But he never stopped. He never fell.

Every one of those incidents only strengthened his belief that Hawk Spirit was with him and protecting him. He wasn't going to be defeated, he knew it.

It took hours for Billy Two to finally make it to the part of the peak of the island where the plateau provided him with level ground.

He didn't think of it in those terms. To him it was the mesa, the tabletop mountain of the American West where the Osage had lived and conquered for centuries. In his mind, it was only one more proof of the presence of Hawk Spirit. Of course the god would move from one familiar home to another.

Below his perch were the machines of the white man. Disgust filled his belly and fed his anger. Instead of the holy temple that should have been there, he saw the missile. In the place of the priests who would do honor to his god, there were white scientists running around, anxious to fill Hawk Spirit's territory in the skies with their vile metal projectiles.

Billy Two felt his face screw up with his anger. He reached down to his belt and pulled out the two boar's tusks. They were blunted at their base, so that when Billy put them in his fists and had their sharp, curving points between his fingers, the tusks were secured in place.

He lifted up his arms to the sky, showing the lethal power he held and making one last prayer to the god.

As though Hawk Spirit wanted to answer him, there was a sudden explosion down on the mesa floor. Billy Two looked back to the earth and saw the first of a series of explosions rending the air and sending a pack of the scientists to their deaths.

He looked over to the source of the attack just as still another grenade erupted. He could barely make out the dark figures in the early gray dawn as they manned the MK-40.

He grunted with primitive approval. He knew who the men were. There were, he was reminded, good whites as well as the defilers of the temples of Hawk Spirit.

He watched with admiration as Liam O'Toole's careful aim sent a series of grenades traveling across the mesa. The weapons were all the deadlier because of the Irishman's perfect placement of them. The soldiers who would protect the missile were cut down in waves by the assault of the MK-40. The bodies began to pile up, one on top of the other. The blood of the guards merged into a common, slow stream.

Billy Two saw that the few surviving men were heading in headlong flight toward a portal that seemed to lead directly into the rock of the island. He smiled when he saw them—lemmings following one another into certain death. He smiled because he knew where they were going. The priest had told him about the temple of the god resting inside the enormity of Devil's Land and had also told him of the other entrance.

Billy Two let out a war cry, the sound of the Osage about to attack, a sound that had sent terror through the hearts of their enemies for millennia.

The battle was begun.

Billy Two ran down the much gentler slope toward the mesa, the tusks in his hand. One guard stood between him and the plateau. The man turned and froze.

There, racing at him, was a nearly naked Indian painted with bright colors over his face, his chest and his thighs, holding up something in each of his fists. The guard was mesmerized and couldn't decide whether or not to act. He was holding a Karlsrupa in his hands but never had a chance to lift it up to aim at his assailant.

His shock was his undoing. The two tusks came flying down at him, striking him on the forehead, breaking through the protection of bone and then ripping downward, opening his cheeks, and finally severing the jugular vein in his neck, letting a torrent of blood pulse out of him onto the black rock of Devil's Land.

Billy Two paused for only one moment to look at the corpse. He felt blooded, like the young hunter who has just succeeded in his first hunt. He had been here before, he felt, standing over a fallen foe, and he'd had a different set of feelings and emotions. He could only vaguely recall the remorse and the other sensations that had gripped him then. They were a white man's reaction to the death of an enemy. They weren't the things going through the soul of a warrior fighting for Hawk Spirit.

Only pleasure burned in Billy Two's mind now, pleasure that he'd been able to accomplish Hawk Spirit's bidding.

The reflection lasted for a few seconds, but it wasn't the time for meditation, and he knew it. He could see, down below, that the three men he knew so well were moving in the direction of the obvious entry to the temple area. They carried their huge automatic weapons and were using them against the remainder of the enemy who were trying to hold them off.

Billy Two moved on toward his own mission.

12

Gasteau watched the murder of his guard on one of the many monitors that lined the inner sanctum of the Peregrine Solution.

"Savages!" he muttered as he watched the painted barbarian use the tusks to dispense with his soldier.

"Is it the islanders?" Knudsen asked worriedly. The Norwegian was standing behind the French scientist and had seen the apparition. His voice was full of trembling at what he'd seen.

Gasteau ignored the question and turned to the other monitors. Some of them were going blank as the grenades from the MK-40 pierced the cameras that were supposed to feed images into the control room.

Whoever was attacking was certainly a dangerous foe.

"What are we going to do?" Knudsen was pleading. "There's no answer from Matali. I can't get Groting to answer. Our masters in Europe—"

"Our masters in Europe will never even acknowledge our existence," Gasteau said evenly. "We will be disavowed by anyone who could possibly be linked to this project. These monsters have ruined it all. They have ruined me. My life is without meaning."

The Frenchman had spoken with an eerily even voice. He began to move around the control room, pushing aside the technicians who were still at their tasks. He was turning knobs, pushing buttons, altering orders in the computer-driven machinery.

"Sir, if you—" one of the young technical staff started to object.

"I know what I'm doing. Do you think there's any other way? Look at the monitors. Those men are heading for us. They're coming after us. You knew what you were getting into when you signed on to this project—you knew the risks."

"What? What is he doing?" Knudsen demanded of the young man who had slumped back in his chair resignedly.

"He's accelerating the blast-off."

"But the missile can't go up!" Knudsen objected. "Those explosions have pierced its membrane. The delicacy of anything like this is too great to allow it to go on under these conditions."

"But there's nothing that says the rockets can't be fired, is there?" The young man's face was full of irony. He understood what the boss was doing, what he was hoping for. The project was dead; there was no doubt about it. But if the rockets could be ignited, their flames and the expulsion of their poisonous gases would at least eliminate the intruders.

Gasteau was taking the only chance he had.

The control room was heavily fortified. So long as the few surviving guards had been able to lock the doors behind them—and they could see on the monitors that they had—the attackers would never make it inside. They could use whatever explosives they had for as long as they wanted. The entrance had been constructed to withstand the same withering rocket fire that would be the death sentence for the enemy.

"I can do it in another fifteen minutes," Gasteau said to no one in particular. "It will destroy the missile, and it will mean that we'll have to wait in here for at least a week for the air to clear, but we can manage that. We have the necessary supplies."

Knudsen was still frightened, but he was also helpless. He knew almost nothing about the scientific end of the Peregrine Solution. He was only a functionary of the business interests who stood behind it. He looked at the one last monitor that was functioning and saw the black-greased faces of the men who were still moving toward the entrance. If Gasteau had a way to avoid a final confrontation with them, then Knudsen would let him take it.

BILLY TWO FOUND THE ENTRANCE. It was a narrow crevice, a single place in the solid piece of rock where the stone had broken apart.

Somebody else would try to find an answer in science. There must have been a minor earth tremor, not enough of an earthquake to damage the solidity of the stone island, but sufficient to cause that one seam to split apart.

There might be other causes for it that the Western mind would accept, but Billy Two knew they were all bullshit. The opening was there because Hawk Spirit had given it to him.

He was barely able to get his large, muscular frame down into the space. Luckily, the rock was smooth, and he was able to use the sweat on his body as a lubricant to ease his passage downward.

The priest had told him that there would be a widening at the bottom. The passageway unexpectedly released his body, and Billy Two fell the last ten feet to land painfully on his side. He ignored the hurt. He was too happy to have found the spot so easily.

The cave he now stood in was illuminated by some light source that seeped into it from elsewhere. It had to be the old sanctuary.

The old man had explained how the Europeans had claimed the temple that had been carved into the rock and made it into their main research station. They had paid attention only to the front of the area, not fully exploring the temple's recesses, which wound back into the depths of the mountain in a seemingly endless maze.

Once they'd been convinced that they were secure in the front section, the Europeans had ignored the rest of the space. It was through the maze that Billy Two could enter their headquarters.

The light would be his guide to their center and to the fulfillment of his mission.

The tusks were still in his grip. The paint on his body was smeared now from the exertion and from rubbing against the smooth stone at the hidden entry to the maze, but Billy Two knew that the magic of Hawk Spirit still protected him.

He moved quietly on his bare feet, bruised from the difficult ascent up the side of the mountain. His entire torso was filled with human pain, but he dismissed it. Hawk Spirit would heal him later.

One by one, the Osage came upon guards, and not one of them thought there was any danger from the rear. They were all watching the monitors, following the progress of the other SOBs as they repeatedly attempted to breach the portal to the headquarters.

They'd brought up the MK-40 once more and now were aiming the deadly grenades directly at the fortified entrance, but to no avail. All they accomplished was to knock out the last of the cameras, depriving the men of their television special.

The tusks were put to work quickly and efficiently. Billy Two's hand crashed the bone weapons into the guards, leaving their lifeless bodies like signposts in the trail of his vengeance as he progressed in the direction of the control room.

"They've left!" he heard a voice say with a strange accent. "There's still one monitor left farther out, and I can see they've gone back, toward the other side of the island. If the rockets can get off quickly enough, they'll still die, though. The fumes will spread over the entire island in a matter of minutes."

"Hell they will."

Gasteau turned and gasped. There, in front of him, was the barbarian he'd seen in the monitors earlier. The man was covered with what looked to be war paint, and in his hands curved pieces of bone dripped blood onto the white-tiled floor of the laboratory.

The thing—Gasteau was convinced it was only half-human, if that—moved with obvious deadly intent.

"No, please," the Frenchman begged. The technician who'd spoken to him earlier foolishly moved to stand between the intruder and the chief scientist.

Billy Two only swiped at him once. He wasn't worried about silence any longer, and he didn't bother with the kinds of blows that would insure stealth as well as his foe's death. The younger man screamed as the tusk, which seemed so strangely like a hawk's talon in the man's fist, cut through his body and opened up his stomach cavity. His intestines spilled out of him. He grabbed them with his two hands, looking at his life flowing away from him with horror.

"This is the temple of Hawk Spirit!" Billy Two said. "You are defilers, and you'll pay for being here."

The Osage began a bloodbath. One after another the enemy, who were desperate to find a means of survival, were cut down by his slicing weapons. The odor of their deaths rose up, and in his mind the smell was his religious offering to the god.

Then suddenly he realized he was finished. Gasteau was the only one of the men who had life in him. Billy Two knelt down beside him and heard the man spit out his last venomous words. "You have ruined the great scientific accomplishment of the century. We would have ruled the world. You stood in the way of ultimate progress."

"Yeah, didn't I, though?" Billy Two grinned. "What was that stuff about the guys getting killed?" he demanded.

"You, too." Gasteau said with weak triumph. "The rockets are about to go off soon." The Frenchman could barely speak any longer. His head rolled to one side, and he seemed to take some unexpected comfort from his thoughts. "The island will explode. The others didn't realize that if it doesn't lift off, the power of its propulsion is so strong that even this place won't be safe.

"You will die with the rest of us, and you'll pay for what you've done."

"How long?"

"Minutes..." Gasteau's head lolled back. There was no longer any life left in him.

"LET'S GET OUT OF HERE," Nile barked the command at Nate Beck. "There's something going on with the fuel in the rocket. We saw some of the guys dying from suffocation and later there were even more just dropping from it.

"We can't take a chance at this. Move this barge as far away as you can, as fast as you can."

Beck revved up the big Volvo engines, and the boat began to back away from the beach. As quickly as possible, he turned the nose of the cigar boat to the open sea. He was about to open the throttle up totally when Claude Hayes shouted, "God Almighty! Look!"

They all turned and saw the man standing at the top of the plateau of the island. It had to be Billy Two. There was no one else who would ever look like that, with a body like that. They could only barely make out the small loincloth, and the paints on his body were indistinguishable at that distance, but they knew their compatriot when they saw him.

"He can't make it!" Nate screamed. "It's too far."

They watched helplessly as Billy Two spread out his arms and began to bend his knees, obviously preparing to jump from the impossible height down into the Pacific near their place in the water.

"What the hell does he think he's doing?" Claude screamed. "Does the idiot think he can fly?"

Then Billy Two leaped into the air, his legs straight, his arms outstretched, his head in perfect alignment. He hadn't taken a running jump, but he seemed to somehow, almost miraculously, get out far enough from the slope of the island that he was going to be able to actually land in the water.

They watched him silently as he maintained his perfect poise and dignity and began to finally fall. Even when he did break the surface of the water—the men would always recount later—he had a beauty about him that was awesome, something they'd only seen in the most perfect Olympic divers.

They waited anxiously. For what seemed an eternity, the Osage stayed underwater. When he finally came up to the surface, he did so in slow motion, like a corpse.

Claude dove from the boat and swam over to where Billy Two was floating, motionless. He towed the Osage back to the cigar boat where Nile and Liam dragged him inside.

There was still breath coming from him, but barely. They went to work with lifesaving techniques. In between, Nile yelled out to Nate Beck, "Get the hell out of here!" and the engines roared into action.

They were barely a half mile out when the explosions began. The fuel from the Peregrine Solution had been stored in many separate compartments. In sequence they ignited, each one sending up a spectacular fireworks display, one that held immediate danger to the SOBs.

The explosions all sent piles of rock fragments into the air, turning them into new and deadly missiles as they began to fall all around the boat as it raced to safety.

The final explosions, the ones that would have gotten them, didn't occur until the cigar boat was much farther away from the island. They looked back and saw the place seem to disintegrate into nothing as a huge plume of smoke and fire erupted on the horizon.

They took it in quickly; then each man did whatever it was he found a comfort to do after such a close call, and they went back to work on Billy Two.

"WILL HE MAKE IT?" Barrabas asked Lee Hatton a week later.

"Yes. Physically he'll make it, Nile. That dive of his left him with some very bruised internal organs and a nearly complete set of broken ribs, but he's going to mend. It will take time, lots of it, and I don't want him moved for a while longer, at least a few more weeks. But he'll be okay."

"'Physically,'" Nile repeated Lee's earlier qualification.

The woman looked at him intently. "Nile, Billy Two claims he's seen his god, spoken to him, conversed with him and done his duty to him. He swears that

Hawk Spirit came to him when he made his leap and held him in his wings to take him far enough out over the water so he could survive.''

Barrabas seemed embarrassed for a minute. "The dive was impossible. I saw it."

"But you don't believe..."

"Of course I don't."

"Modern medicine has learned to be much more humble when it approaches the mystical. There are people who have beliefs like Billy Two who used to be put in mental wards, diagnosed as psychotic. They are the same people other civilizations have crowned as saints."

"You're not going to tell me that you think this bull is real, are you? Come on, Lee, you're the scientist in this group. Do you think that there's a Hawk Spirit guiding Billy Two's life, saving his skin with a lucky dive off a cliff?"

"Are you going to give him his walking papers, Nile?" Lee asked suddenly. "Are you going to drum him out of the SOBs?"

"No."

"Then learn some of the humility I've told you about. I've spent these past days with Billy Two almost constantly. The one thing that he's now even more convinced of than ever before is the existence of his Hawk Spirit, his god. You have a true believer on the team, Nile. He used to be skeptical, he used to worry about his visions as much as we did. That's past now. He has no more doubts. You have to learn to accept that."

"YOU WANT TO BE PUBLISHED, right? Well, I'll set it up for you to do the novelization. We're talking megabucks, friend. I mean, there's going to be a first press run well into the six figures by the time this movie's done."

"Novelization? But I want to publish my poetry."

"Poetry doesn't play in the market, Liam. Trust me." Malcolm MacMalcolm was smiling. "I know how this part of the world works. We're going to make a fortune."

"I don't want to make a fortune," Liam argued. "I want to make art."

"That, too, of course, but first let's talk about the treatment we'll have to get together for the producers."

"I've never gotten a treatment," one of the blondes groaned.

Liam O'Toole looked at Malcolm MacMalcolm, and all he could see was the man who had made him believe in the songs of the Highlands so many years ago. Liam felt his objections eroding, his questions becoming blunted, and his usually unflinching stand in defense of his art was weakened.

Could he really create art in Hollywood?

"YOU'VE DONE THIS just to humiliate me more," the senator grumbled as Miss Roseline wheeled him up to his place at the table in the Palm.

"*I?* Humiliate *you*?" Jessup seemed to be honestly hurt by the accusation. "I only asked you to meet me at a restaurant for dinner to confirm in person the deposit of certain sums in Swiss bank accounts. Also, of course, there is the matter of my own fee.''

''Why couldn't the usual courier do this time?'' the senator barked back at him as Miss Roseline took her seat.

Jessup didn't even answer the old man. Instead he smiled at the lovely secretary and wondered, not for the first time, if she'd ever consider coming to work for him. She had had a nasty streak for him, and he'd returned the feeling, but unexpectedly he saw her in a new light. Especially from behind. Her salary would be outrageously high, he was sure of it, but perhaps there were other forms of compensation she'd accept.

''My dear, the sirloin is exquisite.'' Jessup smiled across the table at her.

''Red meat is bad for my cholesterol,'' the senator snarled.

''I recommend the asparagus, as well—the hollandaise is superb.''

''Too much fat in all that butter,'' the senator spoke again.

Jessup gave up and saw in the woman's smile the vision of an unfortunately loyal employee. How much *did* she make, he wondered?

He waved one of the waiters over to the table, and they all placed their orders. Miss Roseline certainly might be loyal, but she wasn't a wimp. Jessup saw that when he heard her ask for the largest steak and side orders, not just of asparagus but also of onion rings and fried potatoes.

"Here's your money." The senator threw the envelope across the table after he'd decided on a plain piece of fish broiled without butter.

"Well earned once again, isn't it?" Jessup took the parcel and immediately put it into the inside pocket of his jacket.

"A total fiasco!" the senator responded. "Have you followed what's happened recently on Matali? The stable government has been overthrown, and the new regime is vehemently anti-American."

"That's not quite true, Senator," Miss Roseline interjected. "The new regime is vehemently traditionalist, and they've expelled only those Europeans who were involved in the old government. It's also true that they've banned cruise ships and closed the airport to tourists, but they haven't aligned themselves with any other power."

"But to ban cruise ships and tourists is the most profoundly anti-American move they could make!"

The senator was obviously about to go on one of his tirades, but their steaks arrived just in time to stop him. Jessup picked up his knife and fork and, recalling the last time he'd been here, when the senator had taken him away from his longed-for meal, the Fixer took no chances and waited no more. He began to saw apart the well-marbled beef with gusto.

Miss Roseline was doing the same on her side of the table. She enjoyed it even more knowing that she wouldn't be expected to pick up any of the tab. She adored being a guest so much, she thought to herself.

Washington certainly had its compensations. There was nothing so attractive to a good secretary as a man with an expense account, but even more than that, the excitement of being close to power.

More than action adventure...
books written by the men who were there

VIETNAM: GROUND ZERO T.M.

ERIC HELM

Told through the eyes of an American Special Forces squad, an elite jungle fighting group of strike-and-hide specialists fight a dirty war half a world away from home.

These books cut close to the bone, telling it the way it really was.

"Vietnam at Ground Zero is where this book is written. The author has been there, and he knows. I salute him and I recommend this book to my friends."

—Don Pendleton
creator of *The Executioner*

"Helm writes in an evocative style that gives us Nam as it most likely was, without prettying up or undue bitterness."

—*Cedar Rapids Gazette*

"Eric Helm's Vietnam series embodies a literary standard of excellence. These books linger in the mind long after their reading."

—*Midwest Book Review*

Available wherever paperbacks are sold.

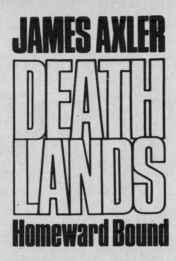

JAMES AXLER
DEATH LANDS
Homeward Bound

**In the Deathlands,
honor and fair play are words of the past.
Vengeance is a word to live by . . .**

Throughout his travels he encountered mankind at its worst. But nothing could be more vile than the remnants of Ryan's own family—brutal murderers who indulge their every whim.

Now his journey has come full circle. Ryan Cawdor is about to go home.

TAKE 'EM FREE
4 action-packed novels plus a mystery bonus

NO RISK
NO OBLIGATION TO BUY